A Far Away Home

Howard Faber

Published by WriteLife, LLC
2323 S. 171 St.
Suite 202
Omaha, NE 68130
www.writelife.com

Printed in the United States of America

ISBN 978 1 60808 051 9

First Edition

Table of Contents

Chapter One
A Boy With a Bent Knee

Shireen waited so patiently. Her mother and father had told her she would be a big sister. She waited a long time for this to happen. She was almost old enough to go to school. "Next year," her mother said almost every day, "there will be

Father & Daughter • By Unknown

a school for girls. We'll go to the school and you will be in first grade."

Her friends had brothers and sisters. She sometimes helped them take care of their brothers and sisters, so she knew what to do to be a big sister. It made her feel important and proud to think she would soon be one. She didn't care if she had a brother or sister. "A sister might be nice. I know all about being a little girl," she thought, "but a brother might be just as nice. He could grow up to be a pilot." So, she was ready for this baby, whether it was a girl or boy.

"Shireen, come meet your little brother." Her dad was shaking her to wake her, because she had fallen asleep waiting. She went in with her dad to see him. He was asleep with her mom in her parents' bed. Her dad told her she was born there, too, and her first days were in this bed. Her aunts and her grandma were sitting on the cushions next to the bed. "His name is Ali," her dad told her. "You can wake him up and tell him your name."

He was pretty little, smaller than she imagined. He had dark hair like her, and she thought he looked like her. She took his tiny finger and put it around her finger. She lifted it up, and he opened his eyes.

"Salaam Ali. I'm Shireen. I'm your big sister." He looked at her and smiled. "Dad, he smiled at me. Did you see? He likes me. He knows I'm his big sister."

Her family laughed. "You will be the best big sister." It

Sister & Bound Brother • By Unknown

was her grandma, Bibi Jan. She was her dad's mother, and she lived with them. Her grandpa, Bibi Jan's husband, died two years ago, and she remembered him a little. He always gave her candy and lifted her up high. She thought her family was the best ever.

As it turned out, Shireen would be the best big sister. She first heard it from her friends. She was telling them how cute and smart her little brother was. They looked at her in a strange way, like didn't she know? They weren't mean, but they said everyone was talking about her little brother, and how sad it was that he couldn't ever walk. Shireen straightened up. She was his big sister, and she would defend him. "Yes he will. He will walk and run, faster than any of you!"

Like all little girls the world over do when they have an

important question, she ran home to ask her mom or dad or grandma what her friends meant, why couldn't Ali ever walk? He was only six months old, so of course he couldn't walk. Like all the other babies in Sharidure, he was mostly kept bound to a board so he didn't get hurt. How could he walk?

When she got home she asked, "Mom, what do they mean? Why won't he be able to walk?" She started crying.

Her mom gently said, "Shireen, they know about his left leg, so they think he won't be able to walk. I think he will, if we just help him." Her mom walked over to where Ali was propped up in his bound up board. She began to unwind him. "I'll show you." When she got him all unwound, Shireen looked carefully at his legs. They both were moving. They both were bent. They looked the same. Then Ali straightened out his right leg, but his left leg stayed bent. Her mom told her then, "Ali doesn't seem able to straighten his left leg."

Shireen stayed quiet for a while and watched her little brother. She asked her mom if she could touch his leg. "Of course," her mom answered, "and it doesn't hurt him. I've gently tried to move it. It can bend more, but it won't straighten out."

Shireen reached out to touch Ali's little legs. First, she moved his right leg. It bent and straightened. Then, she carefully moved his left leg. It bent just fine but would only bend back part way. She was afraid to try to straighten it more. It didn't seem to hurt Ali. "Mom, it's all right. He's just fine. Maybe it will straighten, but I will help him walk. I'm his big sister."

***

Some of the children (and grownups) in Sharidure weren't so nice. When Ali was three, Shireen started to hear people talk about the poor little boy with the bent leg. One day after school, she had a fight with a girl who said Ali would never walk and he was pitiful. That girl was bigger than Shireen but not so big when she was lying on the ground crying. When Shireen's mother heard about the fight, she told Shireen that she wasn't happy about it, and that the other girl had no business saying anything about Ali. That's all she said, and Shireen wasn't sure just what her mother meant. She decided to defend her brother but not by fighting.

All of Sharidure became familiar with the sight of Ali on

Shireen's back. They would go around town, buying nawn (bread), picking out the best grapes, and, best of all, flying a kite. Sharidure is in the province of Bamiyan, part of a high, hilly area, where wind is a morning-and-evening constant. There is enough wind to fly a kite every summer day. Winters are long, with lots of snow. People stay inside in the winter, using paths through the snow to go to another house or store. Sometimes, the paths are so deep people can't see out.

**

Ali's eighth summer had been a good one for Hassan, Ali and Shireen's father, who was a carpenter. The weather had been good for the farmers, so they placed more than the usual amount of orders for cabinets, closets, and wooden plows. A new customer, the new girls' school, was growing and ordered more desks. Because of this good summer, Hassan and Mariam (Shireen and Ali's mother) decided to try to get a doctor to help Ali, but there was no doctor in Sharidure. They had a cousin in Kabul (the capital and largest city in Afghanistan) who might know of a doctor who could help.

This meant a long distance call from the telephone office.

Only the sub governor had a home phone. Everyone else went to the telephone office to place a call, so this was the procedure. Ask the day before for a good time to call. The next day get in line, have some tea, and wait for your turn. The local operator would ask for the number in Kabul, plug in the line to the next town, spin the handle to generate the call, talk to that operator, wait for that operator to connect the line to the next town, and eventually connect to Kabul. If anybody more important wants to use the phone anywhere along the line, you are disconnected and have to try again.

The call went through, and Hassan was soon talking to his cousin. His cousin hadn't been in Kabul very long, so he didn't know much about doctors and hospitals. "Could you look around?"

"Sure, give me a week or so. I'll call you when I know more."

When he got back home, Hassan told Shireen and her mom about what he found out. They all thought they should try to get Ali to a doctor in Kabul.

Ali could hop around on one leg, but he soon got tired so he couldn't go far. Shireen and her dad decided to make Ali a crutch. Since Hassan was a carpenter, he thought he could make one pretty quickly, like in a day. He made it in about an hour. It was a straight branch, about five centimeters thick, with another piece across the top to hold it in place under Ali's arm. Shireen helped hold Ali up to get the length right. Ali was feeling very hopeful of being able to walk. Shireen helped him get the feel of it, using it to lean on when his left leg would take the weight as he moved. At first, it was hard, but Ali was determined to get it right. He could soon move along at a walking pace. He laughed and tried to go faster. After a few falls, he could swing along at a jogging pace. It was great! He could walk! Well, a little bit.

Now, Ali was ready to go to the big city. He and his dad would be going on a truck to Kabul. The morning they left was a cool summer day, when the road was free of winter snow. They said their goodbyes to mom and Shireen. Shireen wanted to leave, too, but that would cost more, so she didn't get to go. She did put in her order for some candy. They climbed up into the back of the truck. The driver started the engine and they were off on an adventure. They were sitting on bags of wheat, along with a dozen or so other travelers.

After about an hour, they went past Bondi-Amir, a series of large deep, clear blue lakes, formed by natural mineral deposit dams, like steps. When they stopped, Ali found out that the lakes were also cold.

Bamiyan Buddha • UNO Picture

Another couple of hours and they arrived at the provincial capital, Bamiyan. They stopped for tea and nawn. This was also the first time Ali had seen the two giant Buddhas carved into the side of the canyon overlooking Bamiyan.

His dad said you could climb out on the head of the biggest one. Ali planned to do just that when he was bigger and when his leg was straight.

After Bamiyan, the road got steeper. The truck growled in lower gears up the winding road. Sometimes the curves were too sharp, and the truck had to go ahead into the curve as far as it could, then back up to the edge of the cliff, repeating this several times until it could make it around the curve. When they backed up, the driver depended on his assistant, the cleanar, to keep them from backing off the cliff by shoving a big wooden wedge on a long handle (sort of like a shovel) under the back wheel. Then he would change from reverse to low gear and go ahead again. When they made it around the corner, the cleanar would jump up and hang on the back until the next turn. This was all pretty scary to Ali, who could see off the back of the truck over the cliff, and could just imagine going off the cliff and crashing down onto the rocks. He just hoped the driver and cleanar knew what they were doing. His dad told him he had ridden on this truck before, and the driver was a good one and knew just what to do.

When they got over the Sheebar Pass and started going downhill, the truck growled less, and it seemed to Ali that everyone was less afraid and talking more. He wasn't ready to talk to strangers, but he noticed that his dad did, and he listened in. The men talked about Kabul and all the great things of the big city. When they talked about movies, Ali hoped he could see one. When they talked about buzkashi, the great horseback game of the Afghans, he hoped he could see that, too. He tried to stay awake to hear more.

They stopped at a small teahouse along the road. It was just like the teahouses in Sharidure, and they had tea and bread. The long trip continued into the evening. When they got to the blacktop road, the traffic got heavier, even including some cars. The cleanar started singing louder, and everyone seemed excited. One more stop for some grapes and then on to Kabul. It wasn't hard to see it in the distance, with all of the lights.

They climbed down from the truck at a busy bus and truck stop. It seemed like there were a million, billion people, people with turbans, people with karakul hats, people with no hats, people with beards that wound up around their ears, people with long mustaches, so many people. Someone was calling his dad's name. "It must be dad's cousin," thought Ali.

"Peace be with you. Welcome to Kabul." Dad and his cousin hugged each other, smiling.

"Ali, this is my cousin, Fareed. Fareed this is my son, Ali."

"Peace be with you. It's very nice to meet you." Ali knew just how to be polite when meeting adults. Fareed smiled at Ali and hugged him.

"Ali, you must be tired. We have a nice meal and a soft bed for you tonight." Ali thought dad's cousin was going to be someone he could like a lot.

***

In the morning, Ali, his dad, and his dad's cousin Fareed got ready to go to the hospital. They took a crowded bus, and Ali laughed at the people hanging on to the bar next to the door. They were hanging outside of the door, because there was no room in the bus. He laughed, but really he was nervous about seeing a doctor because he had never seen one before. There weren't any doctors in Sharidure. He hoped and hoped

Kabul 1965 – Howard Faber

the doctor would say he could make his leg better, but he worried that it couldn't be healed. Mostly, he was silent, just looking at all the people.

They got out of the bus near the hospital. It was huge, three stories high. There was a line of people waiting outside, so they got in the line. Hassan asked Fareed how much it might cost, but he didn't know.

After about an hour of waiting, it was their turn and they went inside. A nurse greeted them and asked why they were there. Ali's dad explained about Ali's leg and said they hoped a doctor could make it better. The nurse led them to a smaller room, where Fareed and Hassan talked quietly. Ali just waited and hoped some more. The doctor came in, greeted them, and asked Ali to stand. He complimented Ali on the smooth wooden crutch. He pushed up Ali's pant leg and felt gently around his knee. He bent Ali's leg carefully and straightened it out as far as he could, then wrote something on a small piece of paper.

"Ali, your good leg is strong, and I can tell you get around really well. I think I know what is wrong with your left leg, but I am not able to fix it. There might be doctors somewhere who could make it better, but we don't have any in Afghanistan. I could try, but I'm afraid it would be worse. I'm so sorry. You are a brave boy." The doctor shook Ali's dad's hand and left the room. There was silence for a while. They walked slowly back outside. Ali was very sad. He cried. His dad tried to console him.

***

Back in Sharidure, Shireen and her mom worked and talked and talked and worked. Her mom was showing Shireen how to make a felt vest. Shireen was making it for a present to Ali. This was a lot of work. She started with just wool, washed it, rolled it into felt, then cut it, sewed the edges, and decorated it with brightly colored cloth cut into shapes that matched on both sides in the front and on the back. They talked about how Ali would be able to stand without the crutch, walk and even run.

When Hassan and Ali got back home they climbed down from the back of the truck and started towards their house. They hadn't told any other people why they really had gone to Kabul. They just said they were visiting family. When they came through the door, Shireen saw Ali's leg still bent and thought hard what to say. What she said was, "Ali, we're so glad you're home. Look what I made."

Her mom exchanged glances with her husband and looked carefully at her sad faced little Ali. "Ali, you look so tall these days. You know what I found in the shops yesterday? Some lemons. I was waiting for you both to make some lemonade. Hassan, you must be tired, too. Let's hear all about Kabul, your cousin, and his family."

"Mom, the doctor said he couldn't help me. What should I do?"

"You should do just what you've been doing. Keep on getting bigger, smarter, and wiser." Ali smiled for the first time in a long time. He was glad to be home.

Chapter Two
Doctors Come to Sharidure

Shireen came running in. "Mom, did you hear? There's going to be a doctor in Sharidure. All of the girls are talking about it. We asked the teacher, and she said she heard it, too. Have you heard anything about it?"

"Yes, I heard there will be a hospital and medicine, too. Someone said they saw a foreigner yesterday, well two of them, a man and a woman. They were talking to the sub-governor and looking at some land near the government office. They were speaking Farsi, so people could understand what they were saying."

Shireen and her mom both stopped and looked at each other, both without saying anything, thinking about Ali.

That's when Ali came thumping in, happy and singing. "Ali, did I see you up on top of the wall?" It was his mother asking and warning in the same sentence.

"Well, you might have. I can run along the top without any trouble. I can keep up with everyone." Ali was proud of his latest trick.

The word was out. There was to be a hospital, and two doctors were going to come to Sharidure this summer. There had never been a doctor. You had to travel about four hours by truck or bus to Bamiyan. Shireen and her mother did not mention it to Ali so he wouldn't get his hopes up. Ali didn't say anything to them, either, but he also knew about the doctors and the hospital before they did. When he heard about it, his heart raced. He did have hopes that this doctor might be able to help his leg, but he didn't want to get his hopes too high. His life was ok, not bad. He could do pretty much everything, and by now, nobody even mentioned his leg. It was just part of life, but deep inside, he hoped and hoped and hoped.

***

Ali and Shireen were on the edge of town, sitting, talking, looking out from the high ledge that overlooked the river valley below. It was a good place for seeing a long way.

It was necessary to climb the hill to get there, but it was a good thing to do on a Thursday afternoon, with no school tomorrow, the weather warm, and a cool breeze from the higher mountains to make it not too hot.

That's when they first heard the buzzing sound, coming from the east, down the valley. They couldn't see anything at first, but they eventually could make out something in the sky. It wasn't as high as planes they sometimes saw, and it didn't sound like they thought a plane might sound, but, sure enough, it was a plane. It came gradually closer, then faster as it got closer. It seemed to be looking the area over, circling around Sharidure. It was far enough away that they couldn't see if anyone was in it, but there must be a pilot. Ali stood up, waving at the plane as it flew their way. It came really close this time, flying over the valley, and since they were up high on the hill overlooking the valley, it was almost at their level. He waved harder, shouting at the plane to look at him. The plane flew out over the valley again, then came almost right at them. "He sees us, he sees us!" shouted Ali. The red and white little plane flew right over their heads, over the hill, and circled back again over the valley. As it flew over them again, the plane waved at them, dipping its wings side to side.

"It did see us. It waved at us." Shireen seemed surprised and not sure, but still sure that it had indeed seen them and waved back at Ali. "Ali, it waved, I'm sure it did. I wonder why a plane would be looking at Sharidure?"

"It was flying really low. I saw the pilot through his window and he seemed to be looking for a place to land. I wonder if he needed to land. Where could he land? He could land on this hill because it's pretty long. I wonder how big of a place he needs. His plane isn't too big. Shireen, did you know I want to be a pilot? I always have, but now I really want to be a pilot. I want to fly like a bird and go to far away places. No one will know one of my legs is bent. It won't make any difference when I am flying."

"Well, when you are a pilot, I want to go with you to those far away places. Our teacher told us about the pyramids of the kings of Egypt, and there were pictures in our book of those pyramids. She also told us about a tower in Paris in France and how you could go in a lift all the way to the top. There was a picture of that, too."

"First you have to see the Buddhas in Bamiyan and the tall buildings in Kabul. We can go there by bus. I don't think you can go on a truck, but let's go find out about the plane. Maybe someone will know. Maybe dad or mom will know. Come on." Shireen and Ali ran down to town. Their world had just gotten bigger.

***

Tent Hospital · By Unknown

They came in a bus, but it wasn't like a normal Afghan bus. It had a place for sleeping, not very many seats, and lots of boxes and packages. Ali found all that out from his friends and from looking himself. It also had people, outsiders (foreigners). They seemed busy, setting up several tents. Now, tents weren't anything new in Sharidure. Every year the Afghan nomads set up their tents outside the town, where there was grass for their goats and sheep. These tents looked a little different.

Ali wondered about the tents. Were they for these people to live in for a while and then move on? He heard the doctor would stay in Sharidure, not move on. Why were there tents? Tents were for people who moved all the time, like the nomads.

Boys Getting Medicine • By Rex Blumhagen

Soon he found out. The tents were for seeing sick people, whoever needed to see a doctor. There was a men's tent, where the men saw a male doctor, and there was a women's tent, where women saw a female doctor. That was a good way, an Afghan way. There was another tent where people got medicine. Shireen and Ali wondered if medicine could help Ali's leg. They doubted it could.

Later that summer the work would start on a hospital. Now that would be something great. Imagine, a hospital in their town! Ali wondered if it would be huge, like the hospital in Kabul. It didn't look like it, from the work so far.

One evening Ali ran into one of the doctors. He had been playing with his friends on the edge of town, and the doctor was running on the road into town. Ali saw him and ventured over to get a closer look. The doctor stopped and waved to him, so he waved back and went closer. They shook hands and exchanged polite greetings. Ali never talked to an outsider before. He was glad this visitor spoke his language. They asked each other what their names were. He found out the doctor's name was Doctor Hagel. That was an unusual name, but Ali didn't say that. He just smiled and said it to himself so he could remember it.

That night when he told his family about meeting Dr. Hagel, his father said he too met the doctor, and they talked about working on an airfield for a plane. Shireen and Ali both interrupted him to tell about the plane they saw up by the hill, and how they thought the pilot was looking for a place for an airfield. Father thought they were right.

What the doctor wanted was for the people of Sharidure to build an airstrip for the plane, so it could bring medicine to town, or take really sick people to Kabul. He said the plane could fly to Kabul in one hour, though it took fifteen hours by road. Dad said the site the pilot picked out was on the hill on the edge of town, just where Shireen and Ali saw the plane. The pilot was coming to Sharidure tomorrow to lay out the airfield. He would need help to put marks at the edges and to tell someone how to start making it smooth. He also needed to get the word out to the people in the area to do the work on the airfield. Dad said he was telling all the shopkeepers in town. The police chief was sending soldiers to all the people in the nearby area to come help on the airfield. Everyone was to bring a shovel or pick to loosen and level the dirt. Ali was trying to think of a way he could help. So was Shireen.

Chapter Three
An Airfield and a Hospital

The next day, just as promised, the pilot came in a pickup truck. He had a big iron drag in the back to make the ground smooth. Ali was one of the first to meet the pilot, and quickly told him that he and Shireen had seen the airplane last week. He asked if the pilot waved the plane's wings. The pilot said that he saw them on the hill and that, yes, he waved his wings. Ali laughed and danced around because he was right, the plane waved at them. The pilot asked what his name was, and Ali asked what the pilot's name was. It was Dan, an easy name to say. Dan asked if Ali could help him.

"Yes, of course, I would be glad to help. What can I do?"

"First, could you ride with me to show me where that hill is?" Ali climbed into the pickup, pointed the way, and they drove away. All of the other boys were envious and wished they were riding in the pickup, so of course, ran along behind. When they got up on the hill, Dan stopped the pickup and got out. Ali climbed down and followed along to the edge of the cliff. It was a long way down to the valley below. Dan started putting out marks of chalk as he walked back up the hill. He told Ali that the chalk would wash away if it rained, so he asked if someone could put stones along the edges to mark out the airfield. Ali couldn't believe that he would get to help on the airfield. By then, the other boys of Sharidure made it up the hill. Ali told them about marking the edges with stones, and he would show them where the edges were. They were impressed and started calling him "boshee," or boss. He just laughed and suggested they could get the stones from where the airfield would be, because the stones would have to be removed anyway.

The pilot was leaving tomorrow for Kabul. He marked out the airfield and told Ali more about how to work on it, and that he would come back when it was almost finished to inspect it to see if it was smooth enough to land and take off. He explained the "drag" could be used to level off and smooth the dirt. He said it could be pulled by horses. Ali didn't say anything, but he was thinking there were almost no horses here in Sharidure, and they only were used for riding. The pulling animals here were cows, used for plowing or threshing the wheat.

***

The next day some men came to work on the airfield, maybe ten or twelve, bringing shovels and picks, and worked a while on the upper end. Ali marked out the outside edges with stones. The process was to fill in holes with stones and dirt. It was going to be a long job. They hadn't realized how big the field needed to be. It was about as long as their whole town. They talked about how big it was, and they couldn't believe it needed to be that long. Most had never been in or near a plane, only seeing them flying high overhead, so high no one could really tell how big they were. They also didn't really believe doctors were going to stay in Sharidure, but they hoped it was true.

The next day only five men came, so Ali was worried the field would never be built. He tried to tell the men that the doctors would really stay and that the pilot and his plane would come if the field was finished. The next day only three men came to work on the airfield.

That night Ali went to talk to the doctors about the airfield, waiting until they finished their work and an evening meal. He knew they often took walks in the evening, and pretty soon they came out to walk. He went quietly up to them and greeted them, "Peace be with you."

"And peace be with you," they answered. "How are you? Are you well? How is your family?"

"We are fine, thank you," answered Ali. He didn't want to bother them, but he was worried about the airfield, so he told them about how the pilot, Mr. Dan, had shown him how to work on the airfield and how there were fewer men coming to work on it each day, and it might never be finished.

"So, Ali, what should we do to get more people to work?" asked the lady doctor.

"Could the pilot fly over the field to show the people that he really is going to fly here? Then people would know he really is coming."

"That's a good idea, Ali." Both doctors talked about it in their language, so Ali couldn't understand what they were saying. "Ali, we have a radio to talk to the pilot, and will call him tonight to see if he can fly here. Come on, walk back to our house, and we'll call him."

***

As they walked they asked him about his family. Ali told them his dad was a carpenter, how good a cook his mom was, and how his sister was really good at school. He noticed they were looking sideways at his leg. He told them his leg was ok, and that he didn't mind if they asked about it or looked at it. So, they stopped and asked him if he hurt it and how it got that way. He told them he was born that way. He also told them how he and his dad went to Kabul and saw the doctor, and how the doctor couldn't help him. They said they would like to look more closely at his leg, so he pulled up his pant leg, and they examined it. They talked some to each other, again in their language, so Ali couldn't tell what they were saying.

"Can you straighten it more?"

"No, it always stays just like this."

"Ali, we would like you to come to see us in our bus hospital when you can. We'll take a closer look at it then."

Ali smiled a shy, hopeful smile. He hoped, maybe ....

They went in their bus - house, inviting him to climb the steps inside. It was a strange, wonderful place, full of things he knew and things he didn't. They went to the radio and talked into it. Soon, he heard a voice that sounded a lot like the pilot. The talking went on for a while. "Ali, he's coming in the morning, flying. He thinks it's a good idea, too."

**

When Ali went back home, he couldn't wait to tell his family. They were surprised and not sure the plane would really come. Like everyone else in Sharidure, they weren't ready to believe that their town really would have doctors and medicine and even an airfield. Shireen did believe and assured Ali that her friends would be out there to watch for the plane and, maybe, their families.

The doctors said the plane would come in the morning. When Ali and Shireen got to school, they told their teachers the pilot and plane were coming that morning, and their parents had given them permission to go to the hill (airfield) to wait. Their classmates overheard and begged to go, too, so their teachers asked the principals and they agreed the children could go, because, after all, an airplane had never come to Sharidure before. All of the students in both schools (Ali went to a boys' school and Shireen went to a girls' school) were allowed to go. It was a true field (airfield) trip. History was being made.

The ten men who were working on the field and all of the children and teachers and two principals waited for the airplane. They talked about how big the plane would be, how high it would be, how fast it would be going, and how a plane could fly. Nobody really knew the answers, though one of the principals tried to explain how a plane could fly. Someone shouted, "I can hear it!" Everyone was quiet, hoping to hear something that might be a plane.

Soon everyone could hear a buzzing noise, gradually getting louder. It was coming! It was coming from the east, so it was necessary to squint into the sun to see it. Then, a shape came out of the sun, lower than the sun. It was coming! First it flew high over them, then circled back, lower and lower. Because they were up on a hill, it wasn't much higher than they were. It was red and white, with two wheels on the front. (Actually it also had a small wheel on the tail, but they couldn't see that yet.) The wings were as big as the middle.

Someone shouted that it was going to land, but Ali knew it couldn't land yet, because the runway was too rough. It was going to fly low over the airfield. It came from the valley, over the end, low enough to see the pilot waving at them. He dropped something out of his window as he zoomed past them and up over the high end of the runway. One of the men working on the field picked up whatever he dropped. All of the students, teachers, and principals were waiting at the edge of the runway. Ali told the teachers they shouldn't go onto the runway because the pilot wanted it to be smooth and not a pathway for people.

Just then the plane approached again from the valley end, even lower than before. People shouted he was going to land. He didn't but waved again. He seemed to be sort of trying out the airfield, getting used to it. When he flew on past the field, the man brought the rock and papers (that's what the pilot dropped) to the principals. One of the papers was a letter to the doctors. It was from America. On it were the words "Air Mail." Being dropped from a plane was truly "air mail." The other paper was a letter to, you guessed it, Ali. It was from the pilot, in English. Ali's principal read it to Ali, because he could read English. It said the airfield had a good start, and asked Ali and other volunteers to keep working on it. As soon as it was ready, he would fly in and land.

The plane started back to Kabul, waving its wings one last time as it flew down the valley. The principals called off school for the day and asked anyone who had a pick or shovel to come back to help on the airfield. About a hundred did, so the dirt flew. They made a lot of progress that day. The next day, about four hundred men came to work on the airfield. Everyone saw the plane and now believed the plane and hospital were really coming. The boys' school had two shifts. Ali was a morning student so he could come to work on the airfield in the afternoons.

Ali and his dad were figuring out how to get the drag up to the airfield. It was really heavy. They put it on the back of a gaudi, a two-wheeled cart usually used to carry people. The horse struggled to get it up the hill. They unloaded it on the low end, near the cliff. The plan was for a team of cows to pull it, so they brought a team of cows with wooden yoghs (a sort of collar) that fit on the cows' necks. When the team of cows was hitched, the owner urged the cows to pull. They tried, but the drag was too heavy. They couldn't pull it. "It was a good idea, but your drag won't work. It needs a truck to pull it." The owner of the team of cows was giving up.

Ali thought about it for a while, then thought about a picture that he saw in his social studies book about America. The picture was of horses pulling a wagon, four horses. So, why couldn't four cows be used to pull their drag? "Dad, could we get another team of cows?"

"Maybe, but why would we want another team? They won't be any stronger than this team. It's the best team around."

Ali knew he shouldn't argue with his dad, but this was important, and he was sure it could work. "I saw a picture of four horses pulling a plow. Why wouldn't it work with cows?"

"OK, let's try it. I'll find another team. You get the hitch ready." Hassan left to find another team. Ali went down to town to find a long rope. When he got back, he figured out the length that would work with two teams of cows. Soon, Hassan returned with another team. The men there laughed at him and asked each other if they had ever seen two teams working to pull one of anything. No one had. Ali hoped his idea would work. The teams' owners lined up their teams. Ali attached the pulling rope to the two yoghs. The cows pulled, the drag moved, and they were off. The only problem was keeping the two teams going in the same direction. Ali solved that by putting a man on the outside of each cow, directing them by keeping a hand on the outside horn of each cow. The drag worked like a road grader, leveling out the ground. Once in a while it would catch a rock and drag it. Hassan started walking behind it, lifting the back to let the rock out.

The local commandant organized his police to lead groups of workers on different sections of the field. First a group of pick-wielding men would loosen up the dirt and dig out rocks. Then shovel-wielding men would follow, leveling out, and filling in holes. The drag was the final step, making the surface level and smooth. As the drag went by, the men in that area would stop and cheer, "Wah, wah!" This was followed by admiring looks, filled with pride at what they were accomplishing. At the end of the day, almost one-fourth of the future airfield was looking a lot smoother.

After five days, the field looked great, all leveled, all stones out of sight, buried, or at the edge. Ali wasn't sure, but he thought it might be ready for the airplane, so he talked to the doctors. They radioed the pilot, and he agreed to come up by pickup to see if it was ready. He got there the next evening and immediately went to see the airfield. He came by pickup and used the pickup to test out the field. Takeoff speed was seventy-five miles per hour, so he drove at seventy-five miles per hour. It was pretty bumpy. What looked so level wasn't so smooth at seventy-five. Ali and Hassan rode in the pickup with him, and they were worried it might not be smooth enough for the plane. Dan, the pilot, tried it several times, looking for the best path. The field was plenty wide. He also measured the length, and seemed satisfied. He told them he had to land and take off one way. That wasn't exactly the best. It would be great to be a two-way strip, but there was no way to do that. Because it was uphill, it did help him land and take off. He would land going uphill, so that helped to slow him down. He would take off downhill, which would help him speed up to get the plane in the air faster. He told them the plane would have power to carry three other people with him. The first flight would be the day after tomorrow! Ali ran to be the first to tell everybody.

***

The plane was coming at ten o'clock, and everyone was going to be there. The governor was coming, too. School was out for the day. Sharidure was going to have an airfield, a plane, doctors, and a hospital! This was the biggest day in the history of the town. Sure enough, right at ten, someone heard the buzz of a plane. Everyone looked down the valley. The commandant and his police made one last check to be sure no one was on the runway. The red and white plane flew over once, then circled lower, and came directly at the runway from the valley end. It came almost to the ground but skimmed up over the hill and circled around to the valley again. It approached again and eased its front wheels

© Don Beiter

down on the field. It slowed gradually, stopping after rolling to the very top, and turned around to face down the hill.

The pilot stepped out and climbed down, heading for the crowd. Everyone cheered.

The governor stepped out to greet the pilot. They shook

40

hands and exchanged greetings. The governor made a short speech about the future hopes for Sharidure, Afghanistan, and for the children. It was all very positive, very hopeful, very satisfying. Then the pilot said he wanted to give the governor, the commandant, and the local Qauzi (Islamic judge) a ride in the plane. They walked up to the plane and Dan helped them up. There was a little step halfway up to the door. The governor sat on the seat beside the pilot, the commandant and Qauzi sat behind them. The pilot taxied back up to the top of the hill and turned to speed down the hill and airfield to take off.

Ali was the one who saw the dog. It was on the runway, right in the middle, just sitting there watching. It was in the way of the plane. The plane was going to hit it and, probably, crash. The plane couldn't swerve because it was already building up speed. Ali hopped out toward the dog. He had a couple of stones and his slingshot in his hand. He swung the sling around his head, once, twice, then flung the stone as hard as he could, hoping his aim was true. It just took one throw. The dog felt the stone whack his hip, put his tail between his legs, and ran across the runway to the other side. Probably no one else in the crowd realized how dangerous the situation had been, but Ali did. He used his slingshot many times, mostly in play, but this had been a pressure shot.

Inside the plane, Dan also realized the danger and had been sorting through his options, none of them good. The rear wheel was already off the ground because of the built up speed, so he could see the runway directly in front of him. When the dog disappeared from in front of the plane, he breathed a sigh of relief. He didn't know why it had run away, and later, after landing and helping the passengers off, he asked about the dog and found out someone hit it with a stone.

There was one more short flight to be made around Sharidure, one for the common people. Dan explained this to the governor. Who would be selected? The word went around, to choose someone to ride in the plane. The people selected an elderly, gray headed, gray bearded man, who was greatly respected in Sharidure. Dan asked who hit the dog to get it off the runway. When Ali was brought forward, Dan smiled and invited him to ride, too. Ali and the older man got into the plane. Dan taxied to the top of the runway, and they zoomed down, then up over the valley, and circled Sharidure. Ali looked out the side window, seeing how small the people appeared, seeing his home, seeing further than the town, and seeing forever. He didn't have to hop. This was so great a thing. After they landed, the older man stepped out on the little step of the plane, raised his hands over his head, and

Old Man for Plane Ride · By Rex Blumhagen

beamed a smile about a meter wide. The crowd cheered. It was all glorious.

Back down on the ground, Dan thanked Ali for averting a dangerous situation, then asked him if he would be his ground crew. Ali wasn't sure what that meant but quickly agreed to be the pilot's helper. He also told Dan that he wanted to be a pilot, and now he was even more sure that's what he would be when he grew up. Dan waited for him to finish, then shook his hand, and said he would help him achieve that dream.

The doctors Hagel promised that when the airfield was finished, they would build a hospital in Sharidure. The very next day after the plane landed, a man arrived from Kabul

who said he was going to start building the hospital. He staked out an outline of a building, right on the main street of town. The next week

© Don Beiter

work started. Town people volunteered to help, carrying, digging, and moving things. It took about four months. Everyone was proud of the beautiful new building.

There were twelve beds for people who had to stay overnight or longer. The most intriguing thing was the operating room. It was lined with tiles and had a huge light hanging from the ceiling, balancing so it could be easily moved into the right position. It was the only hospital for miles, the only one for the whole province. Its name went exactly with Sharidure. It was the Shafakhona Sharidure, the hospital of Sharidure. There was a pharmacy with lots of medicine and nurses to help the people and the doctors.

"Ali, do you still want to be a pilot? I saw you talking to the hospital pilot. Did you ask him about being a pilot?" This was Hassan. Ali's dad was wondering if Ali would like to follow him in being a carpenter.

"Yes, he said I could be a pilot, and he would help me. He showed me how to fly his plane. It's so great flying, and I know I could do it. So far, I know how to turn, speed up, and slow down. There are a lot of clock-like things that show him how to fly that I don't know about, yet. He also taught me about the gasoline he uses to fly. He keeps some here, in a secret place, up on the airfield. I have to keep it safe and clean. I help him fill up his tanks if he needs gas. We have to pour it through a clean cloth, to keep any dirt out of his plane. He's very careful about everything. Sometimes, he opens up the cover on the engine to check it. He showed me what to check. I'm learning some of the things he does. His name is Dan."

"Ali, I think you can be a pilot, too. I think it would be scary, flying in the air, but I would like to fly in that plane. Do you think I ever could?"

"I think so, but I don't want to bother him. He just flies for the hospital."

Chapter Four
Ali's Knee is Straightened

When Doctor Hagel saw Ali coming from school, he greeted him, "Salomalaykoom."

"Peace be with you. How are you? Are you well? How is your family?" replied Ali.

"Thank you. How are you, and how is your family?" answered Doctor Hagel.

"We're all well, thank you," replied Ali.

"Ali, remember when we looked at your knee? I have a plan for how to straighten your leg. I need to do an operation. I am ready to do the operation on Monday. I can explain my plan to you and your parents, and if you want to go ahead with the operation, we will do it."

Many conflicting thoughts raced through Ali's mind, and there were many questions. He didn't dare ask them just yet, but maybe his parents could ask them for him. He thanked Doctor Hagel and went straight home. "Mother, Doctor Hagel says he can straighten my leg and wants to talk to us about it. Could I do it? I never really thought it could happen, but he has a plan, and he thinks it will work. Where's father? Mother, I know it might be expensive, and I know we don't have a lot of money. Maybe I could quit school and get a job to pay for it. What do you think?"

"I will talk to your father about it as soon as he gets home. It's a great opportunity. We have to think very carefully about it. Will it be dangerous?"

"I don't know about that, but I don't think so. What happens in an operation? We can ask Doctor Hagel about it."

That afternoon, even before Hassan came home from work, Ali went to his father's carpenter shop. He couldn't wait any longer, so he told his father about the operation. He explained all he knew and said he knew it would be expensive, and that he was OK with his leg like it was, and that maybe he could wait and earn money to pay for it. He said this with his head down and his heart hoping.

"I have finished the work I needed to do today. Anything

else can wait until tomorrow. Let's go home to talk."

Ali knew he was lucky to have his family. They were always doing something to be proud of. Neither his father nor mother said right out that he couldn't have the operation. He thought they would both want him to have it. He remembered going to Kabul to see about an operation and coming home so disappointed. He thought his family was disappointed, too. But the money. How much would it cost? How could he pay for it?

When they got home Ali's mother had some tea ready. They sat on the cushions and started to talk about the operation. Hassan began. "This is your best chance. I have always imagined you walking on both legs. You are doing so well in so many ways. I think we should try to have the operation."

Mariam agreed. "Ali, you are growing taller and soon you will be a man. If the doctor can do this, we should try."

Now, it was Ali's turn. "Dad and Mom, I dreamed for a long time about throwing this crutch away and walking on both legs. I hope, I hope I can do this. I'm not afraid to do it, but I don't know about how to pay for the operation. I'm afraid it might cost a lot, and I know we don't have a lot of money. How much will it cost?"

"Ali, I can work more every day. The new hospital and the new people coming to town have made my business grow. This year we have saved some money, more than ever before. You leave the paying to me. I am your father."

So, that was it. Ali went directly over to the hospital where he hoped to find Doctor Hagel. He waited outside the front door. Pretty soon Doctor Hagel and Mrs. Doctor Hagel emerged from the hospital. They saw him waiting and smiled and greeted him. Ali replied politely, then said, "We want you to operate on my leg. I do have a question though. How much will it cost?"

Doctor Hagel looked at Doctor Hagel, smiled, looked again at Ali and explained that it would cost the usual fee for operations, one hundred afs. Ali's mind raced to figure it out. One hundred afs was as much as he got from the pilot for a month of helping him at the airfield. He could do this! He could earn it in a month, but the doctors told him they wanted to do the operation on Monday. He wouldn't have the money for about three weeks. "Doctor Hagel, could I wait to have the operation? I can pay you after three weeks. Could we wait that long?"

"Ali, we know you are a trustworthy young man. We will trust you to pay us at the end of the month." Dr. Hagel looked at his wife. "What do you think, Doctor Hagel?"

She smiled and nodded her head. "I agree. I know you and your family. We won't worry at all about whether you will pay. I know Dan, the pilot, depends on your help. We'll see you early Monday morning."

Ali practically floated back to his house. "Dad, Mom, I arranged all the details, and I can pay for the operation myself. It's going to be Monday morning. I don't know just when, but I know I will soon be walking without my crutch. I will be walking, tall, and strong. I'll be like all the other boys. No one will be talking about how it's too bad. It's really going to happen."

When he hopped into the hospital on Monday morning, Ali put down his crutch and hoped it was for the last time. He was helped into the small operating room. It was so shiny, so new. The overhead light fascinated him. He watched the nurse aim it down on him. He breathed in from the cup like thing they placed over his mouth and nose. Then he fell asleep.

He awoke to the murmur of voices, which gradually turned to talking. He didn't know the words he was hearing, but then he heard his dad's voice, asking how the operation turned out. Someone explained that it had gone well. When he heard that, Ali reached down to feel his bent leg. He reached for the ankle that should be sort of behind him and even with his knee. It wasn't there. For a moment he panicked, wondering if they had to take off his leg, but no, his leg was there. He felt for his knee, then lower to his lower leg, where it had never been before. Was it the right or left leg. Maybe it was just his right leg, like it had always been. No, it was his left leg. There was a lot of wrapping around his knee, in fact around most of his left leg. He didn't dare move it. It didn't hurt, but he couldn't really feel it. Was that how it would stay? He couldn't reach any further down. He wanted to see his foot and ankle. Then his dad and mom walked into the room. He was in one of the small rooms where hospital patients could stay overnight. They were smiling, which was good. "How are you? Are you tired? Are you thirsty? You look well."

"Thank you, I feel fine. Dad, how is my leg? Did they make it better? What did they say?"

"The doctors said the operation went very well. They straightened your leg, but they aren't sure if it will bend like your other leg. That will be something that will take time to see, but, God willing, you will be able to walk on your leg very well," said his dad.

"If I can just stand up straight, I'll be very happy. If it will bend just a little, I'll be very happy, but even if it doesn't bend, I'll still be very happy. Can I go home?"

"Not yet, but they said maybe in a week, or sooner. I'll make you some soup and fresh bread. What would you like to drink?" said his mom.

"Just tea, but maybe green tea. Do we have some?"

"I'll get some. We'll be back soon. You sleep some more. The doctors will be around to talk to you."

So it was, his leg was straight for the first time ever. Ali went back to sleep, dreaming about walking, dreaming about standing, and dreaming about flying.

***

After three days in the hospital, the doctors told Ali he should get up and move around, using his crutch to help support the weight when he put his left leg down. Ali hadn't really thought about walking or if it would be hard to do. He sat on the edge of the bed with both legs hanging down to the floor. He put his weight on his right leg, put his crutch out to take the weight for his left leg, and carefully, slowly, with help from two nurses, put his new leg, his left leg, down to touch the floor. It felt sore but was a wonderful new sensation. It was heavily taped, wrapped to support the knee. He put ever so little weight on that leg. It wasn't really painful on the leg, but he could feel pain all around his knee. He expected that and kept a little weight on the leg, then asked if he could move some around the room.

The nurses helped him, and he kept his crutch on his left side to take most of his weight. He was of course good at using the crutch because he never walked without it. He was soon tired and asked to go back to the bed. He sat on the edge, looking at his straight leg, smiling, thankful for this miracle.

It was also, of course, due to the skill of the new doctors.

He looked at his doorway, and there they were, anxious to see how he moved. They came in and asked him about the pain and whether he could put any weight on the leg. They told him they wanted to have him gradually start to use his leg, but it would take several weeks to heal, and they expected it might take a month to be able to use it very much.

"Thank you very much, thank you." Ali tried to think of more to say. "I will be grateful all of my life. You have given me a great gift and I will do my best to use it well."

"We are very happy to help. This is why we are here." The doctors were very gracious.

Every day, first once a day, then twice, and later four or five times a day, Ali gradually used his new leg. That's what he called it, his new leg. After a week, some of the heavy bandaging was removed. After two weeks, most of the tape came off. Before they taped it again, the nurses let Ali see the scars where the doctors opened his knee. He touched the scars lightly, tracing them with his finger. He tried to bend his knee a little, and it bent, just a little, but was very stiff and didn't seem to want to bend at all. That day he went home. He was very happy to leave the hospital. His mom and dad were just as happy. The doctors told him to come back to the hospital every day, once in the morning, once in the afternoon.

After three weeks, the doctors started the nurses working on his knee to stretch it and bend it every day. It was painful. Ali tried to fight the pain. Every day it bent a little more, still not at all like his right leg, but it gave him hope. He was going to be satisfied whatever happened, but every little bit more it bent, the more he could do. At the end of the month, the nurses and doctors decided he might try to walk on it without his crutch.

He scooted to the edge of the bed, swung his legs down, and slowly put his weight on them. At first, all of his weight was on his old leg. He was using his new leg just for balance. Then, sweating and nervous, he adjusted his balance to gradually add weight to his left leg. The nurses were behind him, ready to catch him if needed. He took a step with his right leg, following it by sliding his left leg forward. This was his first step with his new leg. The nurses cheered. He relaxed a bit and took another careful step, then another.

His new leg was getting tired, so he talked to it. "Don't be tired. Go ahead. Walk. Do your job. You can do it." It seemed to answer with some throbbing pain. This was going to be hard, but he would not give up.

Ali returned to the hospital every day, and every day he got better at using his new leg. The pain was less, the swelling was less, and it got stronger. He could also bend it a little further every week. He was now walking around town, getting compliments about how he was moving. He could play with his friends, not yet climbing on walls, but playing tope danda, a ball game where you hit a ball with a stick and run between two bases.

Your team changed from hitting and running to catching and throwing if someone on your team was hit with the ball while running between bases. There could be two or more on each team. Usually, there were about ten boys playing. Ali was a good hitter and thrower. He was getting faster at running, as his leg got stronger. He had to swing it sideways because it didn't bend very far yet.

Once a boy new to Sharidure began teasing him about his leg and his slow running. The game stopped. Ali's friends told the new boy not to say anything about Ali. He started to argue that he could say whatever he wanted. That was not what the boys wanted to hear. They walked closer to the boy and said again that's not how they acted in their town. He was bigger than anyone else and seemed to think he could do whatever he wanted. Maybe he was used to that in his town. The talking ended, and the Sharidure boys ended up sitting on the bigger boy, suggesting he take himself back to his town to his friends, if he had any.

Ali thanked his friends, feeling a little uncomfortable about having his friends having to fight for him, but also feeling great that they would. It's a valuable thing in life to have a friend and even better to have several.

***

Every summer visitors came to Sharidure, the nomads, the Koochi, or as they preferred, the Maldar. They came on their trek from the lower climates to the cooler summer pastures of the Hazarajat. They had come for as long as Ali could remember, camping with their black tents just above the town, with their herds of sheep and goats and with the huge dogs that guarded the herds. The Maldar men would come into town to trade a sheep or goat for wheat, sugar, tea, or candy. Ali was intrigued by these people, though careful not to get too close. There were stories about how tough and ruthless they were. After all, they were not Hazara, not his people, so they were not to be trusted. They also carried rifles and wore bands of bullets around their chests. Mostly, they would stay a few days, then pack up their tents onto camels, and move on to find grass for their herds.

It was in the evening, when their work was finished, that Hossein and Ali were walking on the edge of town, below where a group of nomads were moving their herds of sheep and goats closer to their tents for the night. "Wouldn't you like to see them close up?" Hossein was a good friend. He had always been brave and very curious about things.

"My dad has told me to not meddle with them. He doesn't think they are bad, but he wants me to just stay away from them." Ali didn't want to disobey his parents, and he was really not so curious about these people. He watched them in town, and wondered about their tents and about how they could live always moving.

"Come on, we won't get too close." Hossein started to move closer to the tents. Ali was torn about what to do. He didn't want his friend to think he was afraid, but he knew he shouldn't go closer.

"Hossein, I really don't think we should bother them. Let's just go back to town."

Hossein turned around and made chicken wings out of his arms and waved them at Ali. "Are you afraid, Ali?"

Just when Hossein turned around again to move closer, they both heard the bark of a dog. It sounded like a big dog, and it was not far away. Hossein turned again and started running downhill. Ali started to turn when he saw the dog. It was huge. Its dark shape seemed like a horse. It was close, heading straight for Hossein. It was going to get him. Nobody could outrun a dog. Hossein heard the dog, too, and screamed for help, "Ali, help!"

Almost instinctively, Ali reached into his shirt for his fahlakhmon (slingshot). He always carried it. He also kept two or three smooth stones in that pocket. He loaded a stone, focused on the dog, swung the sling around his head, and fired the stone. The big dog was about ten meters away, running as fast as it could, intent on catching Hossein.

When the stone hit, the big dog yelped and bit at where

the stone hit, right in the ribs. For a second, Ali thought it might come at him, but the dog lost all interest in chasing anyone and turned back toward his tent, yelping, and limping.

Hossein stopped running and looked back. He heard the yelp and turned to see what was happening. He looked at Ali, then ran over to him, grabbing his hand and thanking him for saving him. Ali just sat down, shaken, his heart racing. Hossein sat down, too, but kept looking in the direction of the nomads' camp, worried that the dog might return. "Let's go, Ali. The dog might come back, or the Koochi."

Later, as they neared their homes, they started talking about what happened. They hadn't said much all the way down to town. Hossein kept marveling about how Ali stood and calmly aimed his slingshot. He said he could only think about running. He couldn't believe Ali hit the running dog. Ali shrugged his shoulders and laughed a little. "Ali, what's so funny?"

"I was just thinking, that dog was so big he was a good target."

Of course, Hossein told all their friends about how the

dog charged and how Ali plunked it with a stone. Everyone oohed and ahhed about this great feat. Ali was someone to be reckoned with. He routed the giant Koochi dog. Ali was the slingshot man.

Chapter Five
Ali Learns to Fly

© Don Beiter

Now that he had a new leg, Ali was able to do more to help Dan, the pilot, when he flew into Sharidure.

He could carry containers of gas, he could load and unload the plane, and because he was also older and taller, he could reach a lot higher than before. He could also sit in the co-pilot's seat and put his feet on the pedals that helped control the plane. So it was, that one afternoon when Dan was finished with all of his work, and when he was staying that night at Sharidure, he asked, "Ali, you've been watching me and helping me get the plane ready for two years. How old are you now, fourteen?"

"Yes, fourteen."

"Would you like to learn to fly this plane?"

Ali had been putting the lid on a barrel of aviation fuel. He stopped, turned, walked over to the plane, the beautiful, sleek, red and white plane, ran his hand over the shiny, slick side, then the wing, and quietly said, "Yes, I would like that very much."

Dan climbed into the plane on the left side. Ali pulled himself up on the right side, both clicked their seat belts into the latches, and Dan showed Ali how to start the engine. It sputtered a second, then roared to life. Then, Dan showed Ali how the steering wheel would turn and move in and out. He had Ali watch the wings and tail when he moved the controls. Dan explained what happened when each control moved. Ali tried each part of the control system, to get the feel of how they felt.

There were lots of things to watch on the panel in front of them. One moved as the engine changed speeds. One showed how much fuel each tank had (Ali knew about the plane's several fuel tanks.), another showed how high they were in the air, and another the directions. There was lots to know about. As he did each check, Dan explained what he was doing. Dan turned the plane and increased the engine speed, and the plane obediently moved toward the top of the runway. Ali had his hands on the wheel but was just gently holding on, feeling Dan's movements. Dan gunned the engine, holding the brakes to let the engine get to the speed he wanted, then released the plane to start down the hill, down the runway.

The little plane gained speed quickly, and about halfway down, the tail lifted. Now, it was easier to see, and Ali saw the valley ahead. The end of the runway was still quite a bit ahead. When the tail lifted, the plane seemed able to move faster quickly. As the end of the runway approached, Ali for a moment wondered if they would be flying before falling off the cliff, but he remembered he had watched Dan take off many times, so he turned his mind back to watching Dan and feeling the controls as Dan moved the wheel a little to lift the plane off the ground.

They were flying! Dan kept talking to him about each part of the takeoff, turning the wheel to head down the valley over Sharidure. He tried to remember all of the things Dan said. After flying about five minutes, Dan told him to find a bridge in the distance and fly toward it. That involved a turn to the right, so Ali turned the wheel a little, and the plane responded instantly, his first turn, his first moment of control, his first seconds of flying a plane. He could feel the response of the controls and tried to picture the movement of the parts on the tail Dan showed him before taking off.

Dan asked him to fly a bit higher and showed him the circle of glass on the control panel that showed how high they were. He showed him the number he wanted to go to, then told Ali to fly higher and how to do that. So, up they went, slowly, with Ali watching the gauge to get it just right. He wanted to impress Dan and show he could do this. It was wonderful. It was as magic as he had always hoped, as freeing as he had dreamed.

Dan had him turn back up the valley toward Sharidure. He hadn't realized how far they had flown. It soon came

© Don Beiter

in sight on the left, the trees, the homes, the road. Everything seemed small. It gave him a new perspective on his home town, how small it was, and how it was a part of so much more.

Dan started the wide left turn that would line them up with the airfield on the hill. As he guided the plane toward the landing area, Dan explained what he was doing and why. As the edge of the cliff approached, he showed Ali just where he would set the plane down. He also said they couldn't slow down too much or the plane would quit flying and drop. They touched down just where Dan said, and gradually slowed down as they went up the hill. Ali was in awe of the control Dan had of the plane. He tried to remember each detail of the flight, the feel of the wheel, the gauges, and the speed as they landed. When they stopped, he just sat for a while. He wanted to never forget this first real flight, this first time he was a pilot.

***

The flying lessons continued all fall, usually once a week, when Dan flew to Sharidure. Dan gradually taught him more and let him have more time flying the plane. Ali was a good student. They talked when they flew, with Dan often telling him stories about flying. Dan's favorite saying was, "There are old pilots and bold pilots, but no old and bold pilots." It was his way of saying to be very careful.

Ali's favorite saying, one that he taught Dan was about how gradually, little by little, something important can grow, "Qatra, qatra dareeawe maysha (Drop by drop a river grows)." He was talking about his becoming a pilot. It was true, with each lesson, he grew more confident. Dan hadn't let him land yet. That was the most difficult, but he said that training would begin the next week.

When Dan landed on Thursday, he asked Ali if he could fly back with him to Kabul that afternoon. Ali just grinned and ran to tell his family and wrap some things in a cloth to take to Kabul. "I take that as a yes!" called Dan, as Ali disappeared down to Sharidure.

"I'm going to Kabul, and Dan is going to teach me to land the plane," Ali told his dad as he burst through the door of the carpenter's shop. "Oh, is that OK with you?" He hoped it would be, but he really knew it was.

"Yes, and may God go with you," answered Hassan. "Here, you need some money. We don't want you to be a burden to the pilot."

"Father, I will repay you when I become a pilot. I'll make

a lot of money, and we'll have a new house. I promise to be polite and sound like I have a lot of sense. I won't embarrass our family."

That afternoon, Ali and Dan flew back to Kabul. Ali asked how long it would take. He remembered the fifteen hour trip by truck he and his dad made to visit the doctor when he was younger. "It will take about an hour. We'll land at Kabul airport. The plane stays there. That's where I want you to learn to land the plane. The runway is long and wide. It's a good place to learn."

Dan let Ali fly the plane most of the way. When they got over the mountains and flew into the wide valley outside of Kabul, Dan told Ali that this was the place where Alexander the Great had his camp when he was in Afghanistan. Ali remembered studying about Iksander in school. His army came from Greece. There were legends about him leaving soldiers behind in Afghanistan, and their descendants still living there, in Nooristan. That was why some of the Nooristanees had blue eyes and blonde hair.

Dan used the radio to let Kabul airport know they were coming. They told him he had permission and which way to land. When they flew over Kabul, it looked huge, a lot bigger than Sharidure. When they circled in the valley where the airport was, first the airfield looked small, but as they went lower, it started to look pretty big. They only took up the end of the runway when they landed, and Ali wondered why it was so long. After they had driven the plane to their parking place and gotten down from the plane, a huge plane thundered into the air. Ali now saw why the runway was so long. The big plane used a lot of it to take off. There were other planes at the airport. Dan's little red and white plane was much smaller than any other plane. "That's all right," thought Ali. "It's a plane, and I am learning to be a pilot. Maybe, someday, I can fly one of those bigger planes."

Later that day, Dan and Ali returned to the Kabul airfield to have Ali try some takeoffs and landings. As usual, they first checked everything on the airplane carefully. They filled up with fuel, got into the plane, and taxied out onto the big runway. Dan radioed to the control tower about taking off and practicing some landings. They radioed back that there was no traffic for several hours, so it was a good time to practice. Compared to the Sharidure runway, this one was huge. The plane lifted easily into the Kabul air. "The plane will take off quicker here than in Sharidure."

"Why?"

"We are at a lower altitude here, so there is more lift." This was something new for Ali. Dan explained that it had to do with more air molecules. "You will get used to knowing about how much room you need. You'll be able to pick out a place on the runway, and to judge about how fast your speed needs to be to take off. Also, use the speedometer. You need to go about one hundred twenty kilometers per hour to get this plane to fly."

Sure enough, at about one hundred five the tail lifted, and at one hundred twenty the plane began to fly. Dan flew up and around the airport, then began a descent onto the runway. "I'm going to do a touch and go. We'll touch down briefly, then speed up and go around again. It will save us time and fuel and give you more practice. Now, you take control."

Ali flew the little plane around the airport, moving into position off the end of the runway that put them landing into the wind. Ali started down, little by little. It was really hard to actually put the plane down on the ground because he was afraid it would land too hard. He didn't get low enough so Dan told him to just keep flying and fly around and try again. Ali was embarrassed because he didn't do it right. "Don't be embarrassed. It's just a matter of learning it. My first time landing, I did the same thing." Now Ali felt better. Even Dan had not done it correctly the first time.

This time Ali watched the airfield and his gauges and gradually eased the plane down. The front wheels touched down on the smooth concrete runway. Dan told him to speed up again to take off and do some more practice landings. Each time he got a little better. They did this five times. The last time Dan told him to actually land. He did it perfectly, the front wheels, then as they slowed, the tail wheel, and they taxied over to their parking space. Ali grinned as Dan complimented him on how well he had done.

As he climbed down, two pilots from the Afghan Airlines walked over to talk. They had seen the touch and goes and were surprised to learn it was a young Afghan pilot learning to fly. They said they learned on a similar plane when they joined the Air Force, eventually moved on to small jets, then

Bondi-Amir • By Don Beiter

learned to fly the big passenger planes. Most of their training had been in America, in Texas. They complimented him on his landings. Now he beamed. Maybe he would join the Air Force or even the national airline.

When they flew back to Sharidure the next morning, Dan let Ali fly the plane some of the way. He showed Ali some of the landmarks along the way, the city of Bamiyan, the two giant buddhas carved into the cliffs above the city, and the big lakes between Sharidure and Bamiyan. They looked really blue, and he could see how they were like giant steps, one above the other.

Soon they entered the valley of Sharidure. Dan turned to line up the plane with the small airfield. It looked tiny, even as they got closer to the lower end that looked out over the cliff. Dan reminded Ali he couldn't cut too much power, or the plane would fall. This was a much harder landing site than the huge Kabul airport. After Dan lined up the plane and brought it close to the end of the runway, he told Ali to take the landing. Ali was ready but nervous. Dan was also ready to take over if needed. He didn't need to. Ali eased the front wheels down and kept it online up the hill. The hill helped the plane slow down. Ali's heart was racing. "Bisyar khoub (Very good)." Dan smiled as he said it.

***

Winter in Sharidure came quickly and lasted a long time, about six months. There was lots of snow. Usually the doctors went back to Kabul for the winter, but this winter, one of them stayed, the man.

Doctor Hagel went to Ali's house to tell Ali to be up at the airfield at ten. Dan was flying in some medicine and other supplies. The road was closed, so the plane was the only way. Ali thought about the snow on the runway. "Doctor Hagel, how can I clear the snow off the runway? Dan can't land in that much snow."

"Don't worry. He has skis on the plane, so he can land on the snow."

"What are skis?"

"They are long pieces of wood he puts on with the wheels. They keep the plane on top of the snow. You'll see when he lands."

Ali went up the hill above Sharidure to help Dan when he landed and to see these things called skis. Sure enough, Ali heard the now familiar sound of the little plane coming up the valley. He thought of how nothing else could get to Sharidure through the snow and how easily the plane could just fly over it. He watched Dan line up to land, then ease down on the bottom of the runway. The skis hung down where the front and back wheels usually were. When Dan got closer, Ali could see the wheels were still there, and they actually stuck out a little lower than the skis. If there was no snow, like maybe was the case in Kabul, the wheels would be used for landing. Now this was something really smart. He had a new word, "skis."

Ali helped Dan unload the medicine and supplies. He wondered how they were going to carry all of the things down to town. From one side of the plane, Dan unstrapped another thing Ali had never seen, a sled. "This is how we are going to get the supplies down to town." He began to load the boxes on the sled. Dan also put some smaller skis on his feet. He moved around a bit, sort of sliding and walking on the skis. He looped a rope around his shoulder and began pulling the sled along the road that led up to the airfield. Ali thought there were lots of things to learn about the world. "Ali, when we get down to town, maybe you will want to try these skis."

The next time Dan came with the plane, Ali used those skis to get up to the airfield, pulling the sled behind him. He practiced a lot with Doctor Hagel, who helped him learn to ski. The skis and the sled were the source of a lot of fun for Ali and for the children of Sharidure. Everyone wanted a ride on the sled. Ali's dad studied the sled and made several for families. He tried to make skis, but they didn't work as well as the skis Dan brought.

Dan had a surprise for Ali, another pair of skis because Doctor Hagel radioed Dan about how much Ali liked to ski. Now, Ali and Doctor Hagel could ski together, and it would be more fun for both of them.

Chapter Six
Russians in Sharidure

"Those planes aren't Afghan." Ali was working with his dad. Now that he was nineteen, he was helping Hassan more and more at their carpentry shop. Five planes had just flown over, zooming down the valley, flying low and fast. Ali heard them and looked out of the window just in time to see them. "They were military fighters, and they didn't have our Air Force symbol on the tail. I wonder where they were from." He didn't have to wait long to find out. Over the radio came the message that the Russian army was going to help the Afghan army, and that the Russian people were going to help all of Afghanistan.

"I didn't know we needed any help." Hassan heard rumors for the last month about how the Russians were coming, and now, it was true. "Maybe they won't come to our town." He hoped that was true. Ali went to the teahouse to ask about the radio message. He wasn't the only one. The place was packed. There were lots of questions and not many answers. Everyone was wondering what it meant for them. That evening Hassan got a call from his cousin in Kabul. He asked about the Russians. The answers were sobering. There were lots of Russian soldiers, lots of tanks, lots of military planes. President Daoud and his family had been killed. There was a new Afghan president. Cars and trucks were stopped and searched. The Russians were coming through the Salang Tunnel on the road from the north toward Kabul. The Russians had built that road and tunnel. Now, they were using it.

The first changes were at Bamiyan that spring when the snow melted from the high passes. Several Russian officers and about 50 Russian soldiers joined the Afghan soldiers at the fort. They didn't get far out of Bamiyan, usually patrolling in jeeps, just watching. People were afraid of them and avoided them. The first serious opposition to the Russians came when the principals of the schools told parents that the children had new teachers and that there was a new curriculum, one that was written by the Russians. That made it seem that the Russians were helping the Afghans.

There was also to be no teaching of the Koran in school. The Sharidure principals hoped these changes wouldn't come there. Afghans have always held education in high regard and taken their religion very seriously. They didn't like either of the proposed changes to their schools. They would not support this. There was a meeting at the school about what to do.

The changes weren't long in coming. A new principal and several new teachers were sent from Kabul, people that no one in Sharidure knew. They brought a new curriculum, a better one according to them. Soon the word was out that the children were being taught how great the Russians were and how awful the previous Afghan leaders had been. The children were told at home how that wasn't true but to be careful not to say anything about it at school. At the teahouse and in homes around Sharidure people began to talk about having their own schools. Shireen was asked to be a teacher, and Ali thought he might be a teacher, too. Hassan volunteered his home as the school.

***

The secret school went into action the next week. At first, only ten children came, either after or before their half day of government school. Ali watched how Shireen taught, mostly thinking how patient she was with the children. In time, the number of students grew, and Ali began with the older children in a second room. Although the school was a secret, someone must have said something or overheard someone talking about it, because the new principal made a visit to Hassan at his carpenter's shop.

He asked Hassan about a school in his home. Hassan didn't want to lie, so he said, "Why do you think I have a

Carpenter Shop • By Howard Faber

school in my home?"

"I have ways. Is it true?"

Hassan thought quickly. "If you think so, why don't you come to my home tonight and see." One of Hassan's friends was in the back of the shop and quietly left out the back door. He ran to Hassan's home to warn Ali and Shireen. They dismissed the students for the day and scrambled to rearrange the rooms and hide the books and paper and any evidence of a school.

The principal realized it would be very rude to demand to see the home immediately, but he insisted he wanted to see for himself. After all, he represented the new government, and Hassan was only a small person in this pitiful little town. He had not seen Hassan's friend go out the back door.

Hassan was trapped and feared for his children's safety. He offered the visitor some tea, hoping to find a way to delay him. The principal said, "No thank you." To refuse once was polite. Hassan offered again. It was polite to offer a second time. The principal refused again, still culturally correct. Both he and Hassan knew the rules of this cultural game, and to refuse a third time is very rude. Hassan asked again,

"Would you like some tea?"

The principal wavered. He was still a stranger in this town, and he was under orders to try to gain acceptance. However, he considered himself to be superior to this illiterate villager. He also was more than a little angry about the possibility of there being a secret school. How dare these Hazara have their own school? The anger overcame the orders to be polite. "Stop stalling. You claim to have nothing to hide. Where is your home?"

Hassan's mind was racing about how to explain the school to the principal, but he could think of nothing. He thought about Shireen and Ali and feared for their safety. Maybe he could say it was his idea, and he made them teach. After all, he was the father, and they were supposed to do what he said.

He knocked loudly at he door. "The principal is here for a visit." He was hoping to give them some bit of warning.

The principal pushed past Hassan into the home. He was sure he would catch whoever it was that dared to have their own school. He was embarrassed to find only a woman, probably the carpenter's wife, and a young woman, both preparing a meal. He walked into another room, looking for signs of a school. He even looked under the leeoffs (padded mats on the floor). He noticed one other room. "What's in there?" he asked, brusquely. He knew how rude this intrusion was into someone's home. To even think to ask more was past the bounds of this or anyone's culture.

Hassan thought surely now they would be found out. He didn't know where Ali was or how Shireen and students would not be in the middle of lessons. His heart was racing. Ali and all the students must be in that room. Shireen boldly walked between the principal and the door to the other room. He could see she was not afraid of him. He was surprised a woman would dare to intervene. She didn't actually say anything, just motioned him to look inside. He hesitated, then went through the door into an empty room. Again there were a few shelves, leeoffs lining the room, and nothing else. Shireen noticed there was a teacher edition of one of their textbooks on a shelf. She tried not to look again, hoping the principal wouldn't notice.

He turned and came back into the main room. He had been so sure he was going to catch and stop this secret school.

Now, he was thinking how to get out of this embarrassing situation, although he still thought the school was here. "Excuse me for this intrusion into your home. I had specific information that classes were being held here." He got a bit braver. "I know you have had classes. I don't know how you managed to get rid of the evidence. Just know you will be watched." With that last chilling statement, he left.

Ali heard all of the conversation because he and a few children were on the flat roof of the house. The children left, one by one, so as not to arouse suspicion, each carrying her or his book. Ali told them not to return to these classes until he or Shireen talked to their parents.

When Ali returned to the room where Hassan and Ali were talking, he looked at Shireen, then his father, then over to his mother, who witnessed all of the earlier events. Hassan was the first to speak. "It's not safe to continue the classes. We will all be arrested or worse."

Mariam, Shireen and Ali's mother, was very angry. "I won't have some stranger come barging into my house, looking around, threatening my family. How dare he? Who does he think he is?"

Shireen was next to speak. "For now, I think we should stop the classes, at least until next spring. Winter is coming so we can't have classes then anyway. Let's see what happens next spring."

Ali was very quiet. He noticed his family was looking at him, waiting for him to speak. "I think we can't just let them bully us. Some of my friends have been talking about doing something to let them know we aren't afraid of them."

Hassan spoke slowly. "Ali, they will be watching you. Be very careful. But, I wish I were younger. I, too, would be doing something to let them know this is our town."

***

That night, Ali and two of his friends made a plan. It would depend on Ali's skill with the slingshot.

The next day the principal was talking to two of his teachers in his office. These were his favorites, so they were sipping some tea while telling each other how well they were doing. They were also talking about how the principal stopped the secret school and how much afraid Ali and Shireen must be. That's when the window exploded, and the teapot crashed into pieces, spilling hot tea onto the principal's lap. He jumped up, yelling for help and that he was burned. Outside the three friends ran for the river, putting as much distance between them and the school as possible. Ali's slingshot had not missed.

The news spread quickly around Sharidure. Secretly the townspeople were proud that someone dared to defy the principal, that he had been embarrassed, and had his suit soaked in hot tea. They also wondered who could pull off such a stunt. No one seemed to know. Of course, the principal tried to find out. He thought it had to have been a gun and that someone tried to kill him. He called Kabul to report that, and asked for guards to protect him. He also packed up his things and left on the next bus.

Meanwhile, the three teenagers sat by the river, trying to think of what to do next. They were sure the principal would try to find out who fired a stone through his window. They were pretty sure no one saw them. When it was dark, they walked back to their homes, carefully avoiding the main street and the school. Shireen asked Ali where he had been all afternoon and if he heard the news. "I was fishing with some friends. What's the news?"

"Someone tried to shoot the principal. He wasn't hit, but he did get a lapful of hot tea. I wish I could have seen it. Everyone is talking about it. He called Kabul and asked for soldiers to protect him, then left for Bamiyan. Everyone is wondering who did the shooting. They are also proud someone dared to do it." Shireen had no idea her brother was the daring someone.

"Wow, now that's some news. I wish I had seen it, too. Maybe it was one of the resistance. I heard there are some people who are beginning to fight back against the Russians. Soldiers probably will be coming to our little town. That will be scary and awful." Ali tried to sound convincing, especially about wishing he had seen it. He was very glad that everyone thought it had been a bullet and not a stone, because he was well known for his accuracy with a slingshot.

Hassan came home later that evening and also asked Ali where he had been that afternoon. He really didn't think Ali had been involved in the shot at the school, mainly because he knew Ali didn't have a gun. When Ali said he had been fishing, Hassan was relieved and moved on to his other news. "One of my friends in Bamiyan called to tell me that he had seen two Russian jeeps with eight soldiers getting ready to head west toward Sharidure. He thought they would leave later in the evening." Hassan said he knew someone in the resistance, the Mujahedeen. He thought these men needed to know about the Russian soldiers coming to Sharidure. He looked at Ali, and father and son read each other's thoughts. They didn't want even their family to know anything about what they were thinking. It was dangerous for anyone to know anything about the Mujahedeen. "Ali, I need your help in finishing a project at the shop."

"Of course, father."

***

This was his son, his son whom he loved, his son whom he had carried all those times when he couldn't walk. Ali was also part of a long line of men who had resisted even the great Ghengis Khan when he came to invade their land. Hassan also knew Ali was under the suspicion of the stupid principal, the lackey of the Russians. He knew Ali would be watched every day. He had been trying to think of how to protect his son from these newest invaders, these nonbelievers from the north. He believed God had been watching over Ali and had been part of the reason why Ali could now walk like any other man.

Hassan did not reveal any of these thoughts to Ali. When they got to the carpenter shop, Ali knew he wasn't there to help his father finish a project, but he didn't know just what his task would be. "My son, it is no longer safe for you to be with us in our home. You must leave to begin your life somewhere else. I have some ideas, but first you must let the Mujahedeen know about the Russian soldiers coming to Sharidure. My friend's name is Askgar. I trust him completely. Be very careful. Do not talk about this to anyone but him. He will help you know what to do next. He lives in the last house on the path to the airfield. Tell him I sent you and about the Russian soldiers. May God go with you."

The two hugged, father and son. There were no tears. They looked in each other's eyes. Hassan hoped it would not be the last time he hugged his son. Ali's heart was pounding. He wasn't sure about this leap into being a man, but he trusted his father and agreed something must be done to resist the Russians. He wanted to tell his father it had been his stone that shattered the peace and teapot in the principal's office.

He also didn't want his father to know because he didn't want his father to be in any way involved or blamed.

Hassan handed Ali a small package that contained some money and a friend's name and address in Muhshed, Iran. Hassan hoped that Ali could eventually get to Muhshed and be safe from the Russians. The money was about half of Hassan and Mariam's savings. He and his wife talked about it last night, after the invasion of their home by the principal. They cried about it, knowing it might be the last time they would see their son.

***

When Ali knocked on the door of the last home before the airfield, a voice asked who it was. "I am Ali, son of Hassan. He sent me with a message for Askgar."

The door opened slowly, and Ali bowed as Askgar invited him in. "Welcome to my home. May you not be tired." Askgar and Ali exchanged the polite greetings that were part of their culture. "Would you like some tea?"

"No, thank you. You are very kind."

"The tea is fresh and hot. Would you like some?"

"Thank you very much. You are kind." They sat down on

the leeoffs in the family room. Ali noticed there was no one else in the room.

After sipping some of the green tea, Ali started to tell Askgar about the Russian soldiers. Askgar interrupted him. "I heard about how the principal so rudely entered and searched your home. I know your father is worried about you and your sister. We talked about it today."

Ali was a little surprised Askgar knew about the principal, but then he realized that his father and Askgar were friends. "My father asked me to tell you that there are Russian soldiers coming from Bamiyan, perhaps tonight."

"Are you sure?" Askgar was looking directly into Ali's eyes.

"Yes, one of my father's friends called him from Bamiyan to tell him."

"Then we must act immediately. Ali, I think you know I am a member of the resistance. Your father and I talked about how you are in danger, suspected of teaching our children something other than the Russian line. He asked me to help you get to Iran. I can do that, but we must also keep the Russian soldiers from freely entering our town. I will return tomorrow to help you get to Jungal. Stay at my home tonight."

"I would like to help." Ali was surprised at himself for saying it. So was Askgar.

He turned to look at Ali. "It might be dangerous. They will not hesitate to kill us."

"I know, but someone has to show them they can't just force us to do what they want. We have to protect our families and homes."

Askgar was surprised but pleased to hear these words from such a young man. "All right, we can use all the help we can get. Change into these dark clothes. We don't want them to see white cloth. Dark clothes blend into the night shadows."

The resistance turned out to be five other men, all of whom Ali knew from seeing them in Sharidure. They greeted him warmly. They seemed to know him, too. They also seemed to know about his helping children in the secret school in his home, and about how the principal barged into his home. They talked about how someone shot at the principal at school and wondered who had been so brave as to do that. Ali wanted to tell them, to brag about it, but again he decided to keep it to himself, so they couldn't be forced to tell about it.

For about ten minutes, the resistance group talked about how best to ambush the Russian soldiers. Plans were forwarded, then rejected for various reasons. Ali thought he might know a way, but he hesitated because he was young and just joined the group. He didn't think they would listen to him. Finally he cleared his throat and began to suggest a plan. "What about the bridge? They will surely come by the road from Bamiyan. It's the best place to ambush them."

There was silence, until Askgar asked him for more about this idea. Ali continued. "We could weaken the bridge at one end. No one would see us working under the bridge. I don't think anyone is watching it anyway. We could weaken it so the weight of two Russian UAZ Jeeps would send it and them crashing into the jui (a canal for irrigation or water for a mill) below. The jui is pretty deep there. It carries all of the water coming from the river into town."

"It's a good plan. It's also one we can actually do, and it gives us a good chance of staying safe and of getting their weapons. They will be carrying small arms, probably grenades, and likely machine guns, all with lots of ammunition. Let's get on with the details." Askgar was enthusiastic about the plan.

They trotted outside Sharidure to the bridge and slid under it to figure out how to weaken it. One of them wondered how to not drop a truck or bus if it came over before the jeeps. Another suggested that they could dig out all of the support except for the final timber. That way they could wait to pull it out when the jeeps arrived. Someone would sit up high to signal the others to remove the last support. "But we can't risk calling or firing a rifle because someone might hear it. I wish we had a radio."

Ali volunteered a solution for the signal. "I could be the one to signal. I have my slingshot and could fire a stone down to you. It would make no noise. I can hit the bank just beside the bridge."

The men looked at this kid, this son of Hassan, with new respect. It was a good way. Ali climbed the hill overlooking the bridge and canal, while the others went to work removing all of the supports but one. They attached a rope to it, to yank it out when the Russians approached.

Thankfully, no traffic came during the night so they were able to remove the supports (except for one), and no one disturbed them. They attached the rope and crept around the corner, waiting for the signal from Ali to remove the last support. Ali waited on the hill, fighting sleep, nervous, and sweating. He never tried anything like this before. He wasn't afraid, but kept trying in his mind to think what would happen next. He thought he couldn't stay in Sharidure. He knew the way to Jungal, the next town west, and thought he could hitch a ride on a truck. He wanted to stay, at his home, his only ever home. He also wanted to obey his parents. He had been taught that, all through his young life. He trusted his parents, and knew it must be awful for them to send away their son. He thought about his sister, who also was suspected of teaching at a secret school. She would be watched, but he hoped that even this new invading group would not long watch and suspect a woman. She would be spared and be able to stay in her home. He even dared to hope that by his leaving, suspicion would fall heavier on him and so lessen the attention on his sister. All of this was whirling in his mind, as he waited in the dark.

The sound of engines startled him to the now, to the job at hand. He had earlier selected several stones, big enough to split the air and smooth enough to stay true to his aim. He raised up a little, enough to see the road approaching the bridge. It was the Russian UAZ Jeeps, two of them, just as his father's friend said. There were four uniformed soldiers in each vehicle. The passengers were dozing. Their attention was not on the hills around the road. They likely suspected no danger, no resistance from this small town. Ali's aim was as always, dead on. The stone splatted against the bank near the Mujahedeen, his new brothers in resistance. They heard the engines and tightened the rope tied to the last main support to the Sharidure side of the bridge. They waited as long as they could, until the front vehicle was on the bridge. The rope went tight as they pulled. The bridge held momentarily, then collapsed under the weight of the two vehicles and the soldiers. The bridge, the two vehicles and the soldiers plummeted down to the canal below, the soldiers tumbling out of the UAZs and landing hard in the water. The Mujahedeen scrambled down to them, hoping they wouldn't have to fight, but ready if they did. They didn't have to worry.

All of the Russian soldiers were unconscious. The Afghans pulled them out of the shallow water. They wanted them to be alive to tell about how this little town wasn't such an easy target and how they had been left alive to tell about it. There were eight new rifles, plenty of ammunition, and some grenades. All were welcomed by the Afghans, since weapons were hard to come by.

Ali had run down the hill to see what happened and to help the mujahedeen. In his mind, he wasn't, yet, one of them. They gave him one of the rifles and some bullets. Because he had never handled a rifle it felt awkward in his hands. After tying up the soldiers, the Afghans hurried away, before they might be seen by one of the soldiers and before the darkness turned into daylight.

Chapter Seven
Ali Leaves for Iran and Starts a Family

As the mujahedeen hurried away from the bridge, Ali jogged along, still thinking about what to do and where to go. The group stopped briefly at Askgar's home on the edge of Sharidure, where they agreed on meeting that evening at another home. Then, one by one, they walked away into the darkness. Ali had made his decision about leaving, so he gave his rifle to Askgar, then walked away but not to his home. He headed west, out of town, first up to the airfield, where he would spend the remaining hours of darkness, not sleeping, just thinking.

Soon after dawn, he walked down to the road and stopped a truck heading west, away from Sharidure, away from his early life. He knew now what to do. The truck was headed west toward Iran. The journey was to be three days, made on the back of trucks loaded with bags of wheat, other travelers, rolls of cloth, every kind of item appearing in the shops of the small towns along the way. Greetings were polite, the tea was hot at the teahouses where he waited for the next truck, and most of the talk was about the Russians. When he approached the last teahouse, gas stop, and small hotel at the Afghan-Iranian border, he saw the lights in the distance, small beacons of hope in the darkness. He found out it was called Islam Qala. That's where he spent the night, falling asleep wondering how he would get into Iran. He didn't have a passport, but he had heard that Afghans were allowed into Iran without one. The Iranians were particularly accepting of Afghans who were Shia. Most of the people from Sharidure were Hazara, and Shia. That's what Ali was. That's why he went to Iran, rather than the predominantly Sunni Pakistan.

In the morning, the truck rumbled toward the building at the actual border. It wasn't much to look at. The two guards who emerged to stop and look at the truck asked the driver where he was going. "I'm going to Muhshed."

"What do you have in the back?"

"Wheat, some rolls of cloth, tea, nothing unusual."

"Are there any passengers?"

"Yes, some men going to the mosque in Muhshed." That was a good answer. The mosque was famous, sacred to the Shia. It was very usual for Afghans to be traveling to the mosque. Ali heard all of this and was relieved to hear the truck shift into gear and start forward. He was safely in Iran. When the truck got to Tyabad, the Iranian border town, he got down to stretch and take a look at Iran. He soon realized it was very much like Afghanistan, though with some more sophisticated items than in Sharidure. One thing was the paving and sidewalks. Another was the electricity. The language sounded the same, although with some words he hadn't heard. The people of Tyabad recognized he was from Afghanistan by the sound of his voice and his vocabulary. To Ali, Iranian Farsi sounded somewhat sing-songy, sort of Farsi with an accent and endings sounding more lilting than his own. He could be readily understood and could understand them in turn. There were questions about the Russians. Iran was not part of the Russian plan, at least not yet. They seemed interested in any small thing he had to say about the Russians and seemed to understand how much he wanted the Russians to leave. He didn't tell anyone of his encounters at the school or the bridge.

***

Muhshed was where Ali was going. His father gave him the address of one of his friends there. After a night in a teahouse, Ali found a truck heading there. He was getting used to riding on the back of trucks. It almost seemed like part of his daily routine. The truck arrived in the afternoon, and Ali climbed down to see a large city, not as big as Kabul, but still a true city.

He started out asking people how to find the home of his father's friend. As he got near the address, he found several Afghans living there. It was common for Afghans to live close together, sort of making a small community. One of the Afghans he met knew his father's friend, whose name was Akbar. He was originally from Sharidure and was his father's boyhood friend. Akbar came to the door to answer the knock, and Ali introduced himself. "I am Hassan's son, Ali. I have come by truck from Sharidure, and my father gave me your address."

"Hello, Ali. You are most welcome in my home. Your

father and I were good friends in Sharidure. Please, come in."

Ali was greatly relieved, both to actually find Akbar and to have him be so welcoming. "Thank you very much. I am sorry to be trouble for you."

"You must stay with me and my family. Let's have some bread and tea. We will have a real meal later. Tell me about your father and about you and about Sharidure." Akbar was guiding Ali into another room where there were other people. Ali assumed they were Akbar's family. "Ali, this is my wife, Anisa, my son, Mohammad, and my daughter, Sara." Ali bowed to each and shook hands with Mohammad. "Ali is the son of Hassan, my good friend from Sharidure. He has come to stay with us. He can tell us about Sharidure. Ali, we have had some news, but not for a while. Are there Russians in Sharidure?"

As tea and bread were served, Ali and Akbar's family sat on the floor around the tablecloth and talked about Sharidure. Ali told them everything except about his hitting the principal's teapot with a stone and about the bridge and the Russian soldiers. They all assumed he had left Sharidure because of the suspicions about him teaching in his home.

They had many questions and listened and talked far into the night. Later, Ali fell asleep for the first time in several nights and felt safe and warm.

In the morning, Akbar took Ali along with him to his job. He sold household items in a small shop. During the day, Akbar introduced Ali to several of his friends, also Hazzara, not from Sharidure but from that province. All of them eagerly asked about the situation in Afghanistan. Many of them had relatives still in the towns they left behind, and Ali tried to answer their questions. They asked him why he had come. He told them about the school in his home and how the principal had come to search it. They nodded their heads and agreed he had to leave his home. When they asked him what he was going to do about a job, he mentioned that his father was a carpenter, and he learned from his father how to be one, too. He didn't tell them that he really hoped to be a pilot. One of the men, Sayeed, had a carpentry shop and offered him a job there. "Thank you very much. I will work very hard. I could start tomorrow."

"Akbar knows where my shop is. I am glad to have you join me. Tomorrow is a good day to start, so I will see you at my shop. Try to come at seven." Sayeed was smiling at Ali and glad to help. Someone had given him a similar chance when he first came to Muhshed.

***

The hardest thing for Ali was not seeing his family. He didn't know if they were even safe. He was afraid of sending a letter because someone in Sharidure might tell where he was, so he waited and hoped for some news.

Life in Muhshed was not so bad. He gradually learned the differences in the way Farsi was spoken in Iran. Akbar took him to the holy mosque. He heard about it but never thought he might see it. It was huge and beautiful. Having electricity twenty-four hours a day was a new and happy experience, and he liked the music and movies. He soon could afford to buy a bicycle, so he could get all around Muhshed. Akbar's family made him feel welcome. Life in Muhshed was pretty good.

After two years in Muhshed, Anisa, Akbar's wife mentioned to Ali that Sayeed had a pretty daughter. "She is beautiful like the moon and can cook and sew. She is educated and has a job as a teacher at one of the local schools. Her mother and I wondered if you would like to meet her."

At first, Ali just sat without speaking. He was really happy to have friends help him meet someone. He wondered how he could ever meet a girl, since his family was so far away. Usually, the mothers arranged marriages for their children, so he was not sure how he could ever meet someone. He hoped these families kept the custom of refusing the first offer, and he hoped she would ask a second time. He had been taught that you should say "no" to the first request, "yes" to the second request if you wanted to answer affirmatively, and usually a third request would come only if they were insistent. To refuse a third request is always rude, but possible. It might be necessary to say, "No thank you, but I appreciate your asking."

To Ali's relief, Akbar's wife asked a second time. "She is a very pleasant and kind young woman. Everyone thinks she is wonderful. Would you like me to talk to her mother about meeting her?"

Again, Ali thought before speaking. He wondered if the customs here were the same as in Sharidure. He thought it might be more modern here, and he didn't want to look stupid and uninformed. Already he noticed that many Iranians thought Afghans were "country cousins," admirable but not very sophisticated or modern. He took a chance and this time said, "Yes, I would be interested in meeting someone. Thank you for asking."

So it was that Ali met Nafisa. She was just as Anisa said, and Ali was enchanted. Nafisa also was enchanted with Ali. They met several times, always with relatives present. The marriage was arranged, the wedding held, with Akbar standing in for Ali's family. Ali now had a real family, something he missed dearly. He told her about Sharidure, about his family, but not yet about why he really left. He planned to tell her but didn't want her to worry about anything. He was proud about her being a teacher, and they often talked about ways to teach. She was surprised that he taught some. He laughed and told her that the real teacher was his sister. She asked about Shireen and hoped to meet her. She sounded a lot like her.

Chapter Eight
Flying Supplies to Sharidure

It was his father-in-law, Sayeed, who paved the way for Ali to return to Sharidure, or at least get very close. One of their customers was a pilot in the Iranian Air Force. In talking about what he was doing in the military, he mentioned that he was flying relief missions to Afghanistan. Sayeed, knowing that the Iranians were particularly interested in supporting the Shiites in Afghanistan, asked if any of the missions were going to Bamiyan. The pilot said, "That's exactly where we mostly fly. We drop food and other supplies to safe areas near Bamiyan. We don't have very good maps of the area, so we aren't always sure where to make the drops. Do you know that area, or do you know of anyone who does?"

Sayeed was quick to answer. "My son-in-law came from that area not so long ago. He might be able to help you. Ali, come here, please."

"Yes, did you need my help?"

"Yes, no, well, my friend might. This is my son-in-law, Ali. This is Reza, my friend and a pilot in the Iranian Air Force. He is flying relief missions to Bamiyan and would like some help from someone who might know that area."

"Salomalaykum, Ali. Sayeed has told me how good of a person you are and how happy he is to have you as his son-in-law. He also said you might know something about the Bamiyan area. We are having some trouble because our maps are old and not very accurate. Even if you haven't flown, if you know the area, you would be a great help to us."

Ali's heart started to beat a little faster. He could help, probably more than a little. "I do know the area, and I have flown." Ali told Reza about his flying and landing the plane at Sharidure and Kabul. He also mentioned knowing the area because the American pilot showed him maps of Bamiyan province.

Reza was astounded at this young Afghan. He hadn't imagined that someone from rural Afghanistan might have flown, especially not piloted a plane himself. "You are the perfect person to help us. Could you come tomorrow to my office and take a look at what we plan for next week? We would be glad to pay you."

Ali looked briefly at Sayeed, who gave a slight nod of approval. "If my father-in-law agrees, I would be very happy to help. The people who live there are my people, and some of them are my family."

Sayeed chimed in, "Of course, he must help. He can still work many days here and be of great help to the Afghan people. You know, Reza, I also grew up near Bamiyan. It is my duty, as well as Ali's, to help our people."

So it was settled. Tomorrow Ali would meet with the Iranian Air Force to help find places to drop food and supplies in Afghanistan. That night, he breathlessly told Nafisa about this great chance. He worried some that she might be afraid to let him go, possibly to be in danger from Russian planes. He told her about his chances to fly with Dan, even landing the small plane at Sharidure. She could sense his excitement, so she smiled and nodded, "Of course, you must go. Those are your people, your family far away. Ali, they were my father's family, too. I am so proud that you will be helping."

***

The next morning Ali went with Reza to the air base in Muhshed. He climbed into one of the seats behind the pilots, across from the navigator. As the cargo plane taxied onto the runway, he thought of the first time he flew with Dan. It seemed like a long time ago. When they entered Afghan air space, the pilot descended to a low altitude to make the plane less easy of a target for the radar, and so Russian fighters might not so easily find them. About an hour later, they were over territory that looked more familiar to Ali. He began telling the pilot which valleys to follow to Bamiyan. They soon entered the valley leading to Sharidure. He pointed it out as they flew past. The pilot asked Ali where a good place might be to make the food drop. Ali had him turn around to fly over the little airfield where he had taken off and landed. That was probably the best place. The residents of Sharidure could get there easily and haul the supplies downhill to their homes.

Ali noticed some people walking on the main street. He also noticed that the bridge was back up. He couldn't see if any Russian vehicles or personnel were around. He wondered how his family was and if they even still lived there. He had received no news about Sharidure.

The pilot decided the airfield was a good place to drop the supplies. He flew over it once, then returned to make the drop. The small parachutes opened perfectly as they left the plane, and Ali watched them float down to the airfield. He attached a note on one of the packages. It just said he hoped the people of Sharidure were well, particularly the children attending the school. This was a reference to the secret school, because the other school would not be in session during the winter. He signed the note, "Slingshot," hoping someone would know it was from him.

***

Several people saw the parachutes floating down. They told others, and soon about thirty people were on their way up to the airfield. They shouted with joy when they saw what was in the packages, because there was a shortage of food in the village. One of the children found the note from Ali and passed it around for others to read. No one seemed to know who "Slingshot" was. Eventually, the note found its way to Askgar, the leader of the Sharidure resistance. He smiled when he saw the name, because he was pretty sure who "Slingshot" was. He walked into Hassan's carpentry shop that afternoon, carrying the note in his hand. Hassan knew about Ali's skill with a slingshot, but he didn't know Askgar knew. "How do you know about Ali and his slingshot?" he asked Askgar.

Askgar was reluctant to tell Hassan about the principal's office and the bridge. "Several of his friends told me about his accuracy with a slingshot, but I never really saw him use it." He didn't want Hassan to even know about how Ali helped ambush the Russian soldiers, so if the Russians ever tried to get Hassan to tell what he knew about it, Hassan would never know to tell. "Do you think it might be from him?" Askgar asked.

"I don't know. Maybe his sister could recognize the handwriting." So the note went to Shireen. She heard about the food and how it came to Sharidure. She heard about the note and now she saw it. Her father asked her to look at the note, to see if it might be from Ali.

She read it, examining the handwriting. It was Ali's handwriting, she was sure. She helped him learn to write and could be sure it was his. She looked at her father and at Askgar. She wasn't sure if it was dangerous for Ali or them to say it was his.

"It's all right to say. Askgar is not an agent of the Russians." Hassan nodded to her.

"Yes, I am sure it is from him. I know especially from how he writes his final letters. He always adds a flourish on them. How did he get on a plane and how did he get food for us? Do you think he will come back?"

"We think he went to Iran, but I don't know how he got on a plane. He did always want to be a pilot." Hassan spoke proudly of his son.

"The Iranians have been dropping supplies in the Bamiyan area. We have not received any until today." Askgar told them about other towns that received food. He also told them the Russians were on the lookout for such drops and that Russian fighters were patrolling to shoot down any Iranian planes. "The Russians want villagers to move to bigger cities where they can watch them and control them. They want to make us dependent on them."

They talked late into the night, drinking tea and enjoying

the thought of someone from their village being able to help them.

***

Back in Muhshed, Ali told his father-in-law, Sayeed, about the flight to Sharidure. Ali and Reza had first gone to Sayeed's shop. Ali wished he knew more details about his family and friends in Sharidure. He had only seen it from the air.

Sayeed asked if the drop was successful. "Yes, we saw the packages drop to the ground. I think the airfield was a good place to drop them because it's a downhill short trip from there to the town. It won't be hard for the people to get them to their homes. We saw people, but we were too high to recognize anyone." Ali didn't tell them about his note. He didn't quite know if there could be any way for the people in Sharidure to respond to him or even if anyone would know it was him.

When he got home, Nafisa had more questions. "Did it look the same? Could you see your home? Did you see anyone you recognized?" Ali answered each question as best he could. Then Nafisa surprised him with two questions he hadn't thought about. "Were there any Russians there?"

He said he hadn't seen any, but he couldn't be sure.

"Do you think there might be any Russian planes around Sharidure?"

He paused, then said, "We didn't see any." That was the truth. "There haven't been any in the area." That was only the truth for the last week. There had been flights when the Iranian pilots had to dodge and fly low and scramble back to Iran, but Ali didn't want to worry Nafisa.

Every week, Ali flew to Afghanistan, mostly to Sharidure. The Iranians had been told that no Russians had come to Sharidure, and the towns around there were safely getting supplies from their airfield. Someone in the area was getting out the word that people could get food and supplies safely there. There seemed to be an organized system for receiving and distributing the supplies. Ali suspected he knew who that someone was, probably Askgar, his father's friend who was in charge of the resistance. Each flight, Ali dropped a note, always signing it "Slingshot." He also asked Reza to wave the plane's wings when flying over Sharidure, just the way he and Dan used to do when flying there from Kabul. When Shireen saw the plane waving at them, she now knew it was Ali, and told her family. They never told anyone else, not wanting any unfriendly ears to know who it was.

**

Ali's family grew in Muhshed when he and Nafisa had a daughter. Ali asked if her name could be Shireen. He was at first worried that Shireen might have a knee that wouldn't bend, like he had, so he was relieved to see her wiggling and bending both of her knees. Several years later, they had a son, who they named Hassan. Again, Ali hoped and prayed Hassan wouldn't have a problem with his knees, and again, he was relieved to see both legs kicking and moving. As they grew, he told them stories about Afghanistan and Sharidure. He taught them to fly kites and how to play tope donda. They heard many stories about Mullah Nasrudeen, especially liking the one about how the Mullah outwitted the children, when they bet him they were better chickens than they were.

The children in Mullah Nasrudeen's village loved him and his stories, but they also loved to try to outwit him. One of them thought up a way to get the best of him. They would all conceal an egg in their shirts, then bet him they were better chickens than he was. They knew he would be too proud not to bet. He thought he was smarter, stronger, and better in every way. They also knew he went every morning to the teahouse, so they met him on the way. They asked him if he was better than they were in every way. Of course he said, "Yes." They asked him if he would take a bet about this. He didn't even hesitate and said he would take the bet.

The children said together, "We are better chickens than you."

The mullah hesitated a moment, then said, "How can you prove that?"

They were waiting for just that question. They all hunched down, flapping their arms like chickens, making clucking sounds. Then they squatted down, and each secretly slipped an egg onto the ground. When they stood up, they pointed to the eggs and said, "There, we can lay eggs, so we are better chickens."

Mullah Nasrudeen thought for a moment, then began circling around, scratching the dirt, flapping his wings and crowing like a rooster. "Now, which is the better chicken, the hen or the rooster?" All of those little heads dropped down, and small hands reached in their pockets for a coin. They lost their bet.

At the end of the story, Shireen and Hassan always jumped up, hopping around, circling and crowing like roosters. They laughed along with Ali and Nafisa.

Chapter Nine
Good News and Bad News

When the people in Sharidure heard the news that the Russians were leaving Afghanistan, they hardly could believe it. The Mujahudeen had won, forcing the Russians to haul their soldiers and tanks back to Russia. Everyone thought it would be like old times again.

For a while it was, at least in Sharidure and the rest of the Bamiyan area, but not so for Kabul. The various leaders of the Mujahudeen decided that they should take turns at being the leader of Afghanistan. That didn't work out, and fighting began for control of Kabul. The various groups fought each other, and Kabul suffered. Eventually, a new group, calling themselves the "Taliban" (religious students) got control and gradually started taking over other parts of Afghanistan. For a long time, the Hazara held out in their area, Bamiyan, but finally the passes that controlled entry into Bamiyan couldn't be held, and the Taliban took Bamiyan. It wasn't long before they arrived in Sharidure.

**

When the news about the Russians leaving Afghanistan came over radio and TV in Muhshed, Sayeed hesitated to tell Ali. He thought Ali would immediately go back to his far away home. But, he also realized that if it were himself, when he was still in his youth, he too would probably be leaving for his former home. He would dearly miss his daughter and grandchildren.

Ali also heard the great news, that the Russians left. He realized it would be safe now for him to return. He would make a home for his new family in Sharidure. He would be so proud to introduce his wife and children. He made plans for the return, asking others the best way. If they went by bus, it would limit how much they could take from their home. Going by truck would allow taking all of their things, but this would not be the best way for Nafisa and his children to get across the border and through the many unfamiliar stops along the way. He badly wanted to contact his family, but because the flights now would no longer be needed, he couldn't drop a letter.

As it turned out, the Iranians decided to continue the support flights, to help the Shiites in the Hazarajat get back to normal. Ali continued flying with them, and so he had the chance to drop another note, really a letter. This time he signed it, "Ali, son of Hassan." When he returned to Muhshed, he waited for a letter in return, because he included his address in Muhshed. He wasn't sure how soon the mail service in Afghanistan would take to get up and running. After a month, he got a letter from Shireen. She told him all the news, they were well, and they would be so happy to see him and his family.

He finally decided to go by bus, at least for as much of the trip as they could. He would get his family to Sharidure, then return to Muhshed to move their belongings by truck.

Just before they were to leave Muhshed, the news came about the Taliban gradually taking over Afghanistan. A note from Shireen also warned Ali not to come, because it was becoming a dangerous place again. The Iranians continued their flights to help the people of the Hazarajat. Like the

Russians before them, part of the Taliban strategy for taking over was to starve out the people who resisted. Sharidure and the other towns in the Hazarajat were soon under great pressure. No more letters came.

Chapter Ten
A Surprise Landing

The flight began like all the others, except that Reza couldn't fly that day. He was home ill. His replacement was a young pilot, Homyoon, who made several flights with them as copilot. This was no problem, but the weather in the mountains is always a concern. There was a sudden change, and the pilot called Iran about whether to fly on or return to Iran. It was decided that since they were already more than halfway, they should continue their mission.

The weather continued to deteriorate. The winds and clouds increased and it began to rain. Visibility worsened as they went, so the pilot decided to fly lower, to see if the weather would improve at lower altitudes. It didn't. He asked Ali if he could recommend a place to land. Ali began watching the ground to see if he could recognize any landmarks. He knew they had passed Chaghcharan, where there was an airfield with a good runway. He was looking for a road. He also was watching the pilot, who was sweating and holding his stomach. Ali asked if he was sick. The pilot looked at him and nodded. He also said he was very nervous about attempting a landing in Afghanistan. The Taliban wouldn't be welcoming any intruders from Iran. There had been rumors about the Taliban taking over the area where they were flying.

The pilot asked Ali to take the controls for a bit. He needed to use one of the little bags they had on board for motion sickness. Ali took the controls and continued to look for a place to land. After a minute or so he looked back for the pilot. He saw him curled up, moaning, holding his stomach. Now, Ali started to sweat.

He thought back to the days of his flying with Dan, of loving the feel of the plane, of seeing the world from a new perspective. As he flew, he found he could control this plane, although somewhat larger, and having two engines rather than one, not so dissimilar from Dan's little plane. He focused on the land below. He was following a river, still looking for a road, when he began to recognize landmarks, mountains, side valleys. They were near Sharidure.

As they swept past the town, he shouted for joy. He turned to tell the sick pilot they were at Sharidure, and there was a small airfield where they could land. He didn't tell him that he had landed there before. Anyway, the pilot wasn't responding. Ali's mind raced, trying to remember what Dan told him about larger planes, and how much room they would need to land. He turned the plane in a long circle, gaining altitude for a flyover of the little airfield. The rain and wind continued to fight the plane. He tried out the flaps, trying to feel how to control a landing. He started watching

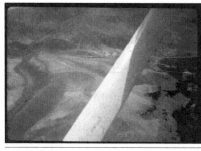
© Don Beiter

the altitude. He knew the exact altitude of the airfield, and he knew about the cliff at the far end. He also knew the mountains and the valley approaching the field. He could do this. He just didn't know how long it would take to stop.

He did the flyover, high enough to be above the hill at the high end, low enough to see the runway. As he approached what he knew should be the end, he could see the runway, and he could see the hill at the high end.

He saw the little wind indicator just where he placed it. The wind was coming mostly down the runway, and it would help him land. It gave him some hope.

The plane roared over the small field. He banked to the left to fly over the town and come down the valley again to try the landing. The plane responded to his hands. It flew very much like the little red and white plane he learned in. If only Dan were beside him. He could hear Dan talking about the landing, how fast to fly, how high to be, when to drop down to the ground. So, he did. He flew the plane down to the end of the runway, concentrating on the ground and feeling for the runway. He had it just right. The end of the little field came up quickly, and Ali saw he needed more room.

He remembered Dan telling him about a time when he had faced this situation and how he ground-looped the plane, doing a hard left to spin and stop the plane before running into what was ahead. So again, he heard Dan talking and did just that. The plane pivoted on the end of the left wing and the left side wheel, and spun around 180 degrees to face back down the runway. It also shuddered to a stop and plopped back onto all of the landing gear.

Ali just sat at the controls, shaking, gripping the wheel. They were down, safely. The pilot had missed a great landing. Just where was the pilot? When the plane lurched violently around in the ground loop, the pilot had been thrown against the side of the cockpit, where he now lay unconscious. At least now he wasn't moaning or holding his stomach.

Ali's next thought was that he was home, home to see his parents and his sister. He started to exit the plane, when he had a second thought. Were the Taliban going to be outside, waiting for him? Surely someone saw or heard the plane. Maybe not, with the howling wind and the rain, maybe no one saw or heard anything. He heard moaning coming from the pilot, who was waking up. Ali went to him, asking him if he was all right.

"Yes, I think so. Where are we? Did we crash? Where are we?"

"We're in Sharidure, my far away home. We didn't crash. I landed the plane."

"How did you land it? How did you know how?"

"I have flown before, a long time ago. I even took off and landed at this exact airfield. That's how I knew where to land, and how to land." Ali tried to sound confident, but not to brag. It turned out he didn't have to. The pilot did it for him.

"I still don't know how you did it, no runway markers, no air traffic control, nothing. It's amazing. I'm glad I was unconscious, because I would have been scared stiff. Let's get out to see this home of yours."

They climbed down. The rain kept on. Ali was thankful now for the wind. It must have helped them land and shortened their landing enough to keep them on the runway. He looked over at the little wind indicator and laughed out loud, remembering putting it up. He wondered who replaced the original one and kept it working for all these years. Maybe some little boy like he had been, or maybe Shireen. It was only a stick and some cloth, nothing much, yet enough to help him land and save his life.

"Have you seen any sign of people?" The pilot was probably wondering too about the Taliban.

"No, but the storm is probably keeping them inside and kept them from hearing or seeing this plane. Let's walk down to the village to find them." Ali didn't say anything about the Taliban. He was hoping they might not have ever come to Sharidure.

***

The first house they came to was that of Askgar, the leader of the local Mujahadeen, the leader of the group that Ali had helped drop the Russian UAZs into the canal. No answer came from the house and Ali was a bit surprised. He couldn't imagine that nobody was there. They walked further into town, but still didn't see anyone. The next house they came to was Ali's home. He couldn't wait to see his family. He knocked, and knocked again. There was no answer. He began to worry. He called his father. "Father, I'm home. It's Ali, your son." He thought he heard someone inside. "Shireen, it's Ali, your brother. Are you there?"

The voice that answered was Shireen, his sister. "If you are Ali, where did our mother hide the candy?"

It was a question only Ali could answer. Even their mother didn't know they knew. What was making her so afraid of answering the door? "Behind the curtain, in the window of the kitchen."

The door opened slowly. Shireen peeked timidly out, knowing it must be Ali, but still afraid. "Ali, it is you!" Now she was the old, unafraid of anything Shireen. She stopped when she saw the other man, the Iranian pilot. Ali introduced them and reassured her it was all right. All the while they were standing in the rain. Shireen laughed and said they might want to come in out of the rain. Ali laughed, too, and stepped into his home.

"Is Dad at his shop? Where's Mom? Sorry, how are you? I don't know where to start."

Shireen waited for him to finish, then asked him and the pilot to please sit down. "Would you like some tea? You must be tired. I'm sorry I kept you outside and didn't answer the door." She brought them some green tea and some warm bread. They sat on the floor cushions, placing their cups and plates in front of them.

"Ali, mother died last month, mostly of sadness and fear, I think. She left a letter for you. She told me what to write. It's a wonderful letter, full of love. She said she knew you would come back. She wasn't sick, just so sad. She suffered a lot when father died. He was killed by the Taliban when they came to Sharidure. They brought all of the men in and lined them up and shot them all. I can't tell you how terrible it was. If you had been here, they would have killed you, too. They came back several times, though not lately. That's why I was afraid to open the door."

Ali began weeping. He was overcome by his parents being gone. The only sound was his sobbing.

Finally he stood. "Could I see the letter?" Shireen went to get it. It was folded once. Ali opened it and read it, silently. It sounded just like his mother, full of love and quietness. He could see her, sitting, telling Shireen what to write. It told of her joy in seeing his plane, waving its wings, knowing it was him, and how proud she was that he could be bringing food to them. There were hints of her sadness, of how afraid she was of the Taliban, but mostly, it was words of hope, saying she knew a better day was coming. He refolded the letter and tucked it into his felt vest, the one she had made before he left.

***

That afternoon, the rain stopped, the wind died down, and the sun came out. The pilot wanted to go see the plane and the damage, if any was done in the landing. Really he wanted to leave the brother and sister to themselves, to talk more without an outsider there to hear. Ali and Shireen appreciated it. Ali showed him the path up to the airfield.

Ali wanted to go into his old town. He went first to his father's carpentry shop. Inside, it was just like he remembered, with various projects left to be finished. On a table was a toy truck, partially painted. His dad must have been making it for some child. He sat down at the table the truck was on. The paint jars were there, and so was a small brush. The truck was a model of the local trucks, a "loree," the same kind he and his father rode in the back of to Kabul, the same kind he rode on his way to Iran. He sat a while, then decided to complete the painting. Just before the daylight faded, he had finished. He set it aside to dry. It felt so good to be there, in his father's shop, in his hometown. He began to think about his family, far away in Iran. They must be worried by now, wondering why he wasn't back.

He walked up to the plane, hoping the radio might work to call Iran. The pilot was in the plane, checking out the systems. He said the radio worked, but that he was hesitant to try to call because some unfriendly ears might hear and get a fix on where they were. He showed Ali the broken propeller on the wing that had been the pivot for the ground loop landing. The end of the wing was also damaged. They wouldn't be flying out of Sharidure, at least not today.

Ali and Homyoon talked about what to do next. They decided that a telephone call was the best way to let someone in Iran know what happened, so they walked back down to the town to try the local telephone office. It wasn't open and looked deserted, so they went back to Ali's home. Shireen told them the operator was killed with all of the other men, and since then, no one could make a phone call. Homyoon wanted to leave right away, maybe taking a truck back to Iran. Ali didn't know what to do. Shireen thought he should go back with the pilot. "Ali, you have your own family to take care of. You should go back. I'll be OK here." Her words said that, but her eyes spoke of fear and uncertainty.

Ali was torn about what to do. "Let's go see if there even is a way to go back to Iran." They heard the sound of a vehicle in the distance, heading for Sharidure. "It might be the Taliban," Ali said out loud. They didn't want to be seen if it was. Ali led Homyoon up above the town to wait and see what it was that came into town. It turned out to be a truck, loaded with bags of wheat and a few passengers. Ali motioned for Homyoon to stay there and went down toward the truck to get a closer look. Some of the older women of Sharidure went out to see the truck. Ali waited inside his father's shop, staying out of sight.

The truck stopped on the main street, and Ali could hear the driver talking to the women. The women were asking about buying wheat. The driver looked and sounded Tajik, speaking Dari. Ali felt safer. Taliban would be speaking Pushtu. He wished he had a weapon. He looked around the shop. In the back he found something he used a long time ago, his slingshot. It was one he had used, one his father made for him. It felt good in his hand. Placing it in his waistband inside his long shirt, he went out to talk to the driver.

The women stepped back when he approached. Ali knew them. He wasn't sure they would know him. "Hello, how are you? May you not be tired."

The driver returned the greeting. He asked if Ali lived here, and what his name was.

"Ali, son of Hassan." Ali noticed the women move a bit closer when he said his name. "Would you sell me some wheat? How much is a bag?" After some bargaining, the driver told one of his assistants to throw down a bag, a big one. Ali tested its weight. It seemed the right weight, the one they had agreed on, so he gave the driver the money. The driver looked at the Iranian notes. Ali wondered if he would take them, but the driver nodded and accepted them. He said he was going to Herat and could exchange the money there, or just use it. There was plenty of Iranian money in Herat. Ali ventured, "Would you take a passenger to Herat?"

"Maybe. Are you going all the way to Herat?"

Ali didn't want to tell him too much. "Yes. Actually, it's my Iranian friend who wants to go. Your truck looks new and in great shape. I think he would be glad to ride with you. How much to have him ride in the cab?" The bargaining began again. Ali didn't know how much it should cost, but he was sure this was the best way for Homyoon to get to Iran. Buses went daily from Herat to Muhshed. Ali hinted that there might be a bonus if the driver got Homyoon to Herat safely. The driver said he was leaving in ten minutes.

Ali bought one more bag of wheat, then went to get Homyoon, who was a bit worried about going on the truck. Ali assured him it was a safe way to get to Herat, and that buses went every day to Muhshed from Herat. They hurried down to the truck. Ali made his own decision. He was staying. This was his real home so he had to stay. As the truck rumbled up the road west, he knew he made the right decision. He sent a hurriedly written note to Nafisa and his children, explaining why he had to stay, at least for now.

He carried one of the wheat bags to his house, after carrying the other into his father's shop. When he carried the bag inside, Shireen started crying. He could tell she was very happy to see him stay. There was a lot to do in Sharidure.

***

First, there was the garden to plant so they would have vegetables in the summer and winter, but where could he get seeds? It turned out Shireen had kept some hidden in the house. She had corn, tomatoes, eggplant, carrots, potatoes, and lettuce. Ali went to work planting them in their field. He thought about wheat, but they didn't have enough land to grow enough to feed them. He asked Shireen if anyone she

Plowing With Oxen • By Unknown

knew had land to plant wheat. She did. One of her friends who lived on the edge of town had several jereebs (about four acres) of land. Two other friends had cows to pull the plow to soften the ground for planting. That is how, the first week he was back home, Ali became a farmer during the day.

Shireen negotiated a deal with the landowner and the owners of the cows to share the wheat crop.

At night, Ali was a carpenter, first repairing, later making furniture for the women in Sharidure. He wouldn't take money but agreed to take eggs, vegetables, milk, and other food for pay.

***

About two weeks later, a truck coming from the west arrived with a letter for Ali from Nafisa, his wife. The letter was full of joy and news about their children. Everything was fine. He didn't have to worry about them, but they would like to see him when he could come.

The letter was delivered by Reza, the Iranian pilot. "Ali, the Iranian government wants me to fly the plane back to Muhshed. They are worried the Taliban might hear about the plane and claim Iran is interfering in Afghanistan. Actually, they aren't worried about them thinking that. The Taliban know Iran is helping the Shia in Afghanistan. It's just that they can't prove it. There is also some concern that your town might be punished if the plane is found here."

"I am worried about that, too. Our town has suffered enough, and I don't want to bring danger to Shireen or anyone else. Can we fly the plane out?"

"Let's go see it. Homyoon told me to bring a propeller and a wing-tip. I also brought fuel and some tools." Reza sounded encouraging. They walked up to the airfield to see the plane. Except for the propeller and wing-tip, the plane seemed completely damage free. Reza climbed down from the cockpit and nodded his approval to Ali. "It seems like it could fly. This airfield seems a little short, though. How long is it?"

Ali knew exactly how long it was and went on to tell Reza the story of the little field. He told Reza about Dan and the flying lessons he gave him. He also told Reza about the wind lift at the end of the runway. He and Reza walked down to end of the runway to look over the edge at the valley below. "It helps that the runway is downhill. It helps the plane pick up speed for the takeoff. How much runway does this plane need to take off?"

"About fifty meters more than this runway." Reza was calm in his answer. "Did the pilot have any other tricks for takeoff?"

"He did say you could start out uphill and get up some speed, then make a wide turn to head down the hill. We never had to do that."

As they walked back up to the plane, Ali could tell that Reza was trying to figure out what to do. When they got to the plane, Reza seemed to have decided. "Ali, go back to get the fuel. I'll run some preflight checks to be sure the engines and other systems work. When you get back, we'll decide about flying out of here." Ali noticed the word "we." He felt honored that he was to help make the decision.

On the way back to his house to get the aviation fuel, Ali thought about how to get the four fuel containers back up to the plane. Maybe two strong men could carry one at a time, but there were no men here. Maybe two strong women could carry the containers. How about a donkey? Were there any? Shireen would know.

His sister met him at the door. "Ali, someone just came from Bamiyan. There's been a rumor that a plane landed in Sharidure. They are worried the Taliban might hear. Is it possible to fly the plane away? Everyone is worried what might happen if the Taliban came and found a plane. They would probably start searching homes for whoever flew it here." Her voice was trying to be calm, but Ali could tell she was afraid.

"Reza is testing it now, to see if it can fly. We need to replace one propeller and try to fix a wing-tip. We also need to get the fuel up to the plane. Does anyone have a donkey?"

Shireen thought a minute. "Yes, I know a family that has

two. Their children used to come to our house. I'm sure we could use their donkeys. I'll go to ask. There's also a gaudi

behind dad's shop. He was fixing it. See if it is usable."

Ali hurried out to the shop. The old gaudi was there, right where Shireen said it

Gaudi • By Howard Faber

would be. He could see his dad had been working on it. It looked like one of the shafts had been broken. It had been replaced, just not painted. A harness was on the seat of the gaudi. He had never driven one, but he could try. He pulled it around to the street and to their house.

Nobody was around to watch him. He was happy for that, so no one would know about them bringing fuel or anything else to the plane. The Taliban could easily force people to talk. He waited for Shireen.

In about a half hour, Shireen returned with one donkey. "They asked why I needed two, and I could only think of needing to carry water from the river, so they let me use one."

"The gaudi seems to be usable, so one will have to do. The shafts are for a horse. The donkey isn't as big as a horse, but he looks strong. Let's see if the harness will fit. Have you ever driven a gaudi or put on a harness?"

Shireen just looked at him. Obviously, she hadn't. "It didn't hurt to ask," he thought. "Well, it can't be that hard." Inside their compound wall, they led the donkey up to the gaudi. Ali got the harness and stretched it out on the ground. They figured out which of the straps were the front, lifted it up and draped it on the back of the donkey. They found one that seemed to want to go over the withers and around the belly of the donkey. It had a buckle that seemed to fit a strap with holes on the other side. It was a little long, so Ali ran to get a tool from the shop to make new holes. It snugged up to hold the whole front of the harness in place. Next, they found a thick strap with two long straps that seemed to be how the donkey would pull the gaudi. It went around the front of his chest and back to the gaudi. Ali could remember seeing this. It was held up by a strap over the neck. It seemed too long, so he made some new holes and it fit high enough on the chest for pulling. At the end of the straps were slits that fit over the ends of a pivoting bar at the front of the gaudi. It was going to work. "The bridle, have you seen one or reins?" Shireen looked again on the gaudi.

"I don't see any. What could we use? Could we tie rope on the halter?" Shireen led the donkey with a rope tied on its halter.

"That's a good idea, Shireen. I saw rope in dad's shop. I'll be right back." He soon returned with a long rope and a knife. He tied the ends of the rope on both sides of the halter. He wished there was a real bridle with a bit, but there wasn't, so they would just have to make it work.

When they loaded the back of the two-wheeled cart with the fuel containers, it tipped back, almost lifting the donkey in the air. They looked at each other and quickly took two containers off. It still tipped back, but not so much.

"Maybe if one of us sat in the front it would balance the load. Why don't you try it," she suggested. Ali got in the front. It was much better. Shireen opened the gate of the compound and led the donkey out. Ali pulled on the right rein to turn up the street. The donkey just stopped. Shireen went up to him and led him in the right direction. She looked at Ali and just shrugged and grinned. "It could be worse. He's pulling the load."

It turned out to be fun. They hadn't worked together on anything for such a long time. When they got up to the airfield, Reza stepped down from the plane and directed them around to the fuel tanks on one wing. Ali handed up the container, and Reza poured it into a tank. He was careful to strain it through a cloth. They didn't need any fuel problems. Ali handed up the second container, and he and Shireen turned back down to the town to get the other containers. This trip Ali led, and Shireen got to ride. It was only fair.

There was one more trip needed to bring up the propeller and parts for the wing-tip. Ali and Reza sweated to remove the damaged propeller, and it was even harder to lift up and bolt on the new one. The wing-tip was worse than Reza thought, but they did manage to get on the new parts and make the surface smooth enough for Reza to think it would stay together. As they returned down to the town, with Shireen and Reza riding, they talked about when the best time would be for Reza to fly out. It was decided he would leave in the morning.

Shireen went to see if anyone knew any more about the Taliban coming.

Chapter Eleven
The Taliban Are Coming

She was back in ten minutes, running, out of breath. "The Taliban are coming." Her eyes were wide with fright. "One of my friends just came on the bus from Bamiyan. They passed Taliban in pickups at Bondi-Amir. The Taliban stopped to eat there. The bus driver didn't stop at all for fear the Taliban would search the bus or just harass them. They must be coming here, because there's no other town on the road. Ali, you have to leave and fly the plane out, now!"

Ali jumped to his feet and ran outside, then came back in to say goodbye to his sister. Both were crying. It might be the last time they saw each other. Then he ran up the path to the airfield. When he got there, he yelled to Reza that they had to leave now, because the Taliban were coming.

Reza didn't say anything; he just climbed up into the

plane. He shouted to Ali to remove the chocks that anchored the plane where it sat. Ali did that and was just about to climb up when he thought about something that would be just as deadly to the people of Sharidure as the plane itself, the tracks. The plane would leave tracks as it sped down the runway. Reza waved to him to get aboard, but Ali just waved back and pointed to the town. He would have to stay behind. Reza shrugged and turned the plane uphill, according to their plan to gain as much speed as possible. Ali ran over to the small building at the top of the runway, hoping there might be a broom inside.

Reza turned the plane around at the top of the runway, trying to maintain as much speed as possible. The engines and propellers roared, pulling the plane down the runway. The plane surged forward. Ali just hoped it would be going fast enough at the end of the runway. Maybe, the light load (no supplies and only one person) would help it get airborne. Meanwhile, he did find a broom, one of the local jaru, handmade, just right for a fast sweep. He started sweeping out the tracks of the plane at the top of the runway.

He stopped to watch when the plane got to the end of

the runway, to the edge of the cliff overlooking the river valley. His heart stopped as it disappeared off the edge, dropping down below the edge of the cliff. He ran to see it smashed into the valley, a terrible sight, one that would not only doom Reza but also the people of Sharidure. The Taliban would know a plane from Iran had been here, and would search and threaten until he and his sister were found. Then he stopped, because just as it had disappeared, it rose into view, first level with the runway, then gradually rising higher, turning west toward Iran, out of sight of the Taliban. He stopped a moment to thank God. He also spoke a brief prayer for his sister's safety. The Taliban might have already arrived in town, possibly hearing and seeing the plane.

He ran back to where he left off sweeping away the tracks of the plane. He kept hoping that the Taliban had not come in time, hoping he would have time to sweep away the tracks. He also kept looking over his shoulder toward the path down to the town. His arms were getting tired, but the thought of the black-turbaned Taliban finding him drove him on. At last, he approached the cliff where the last of the tracks disappeared at the edge. That's when he heard the sound of engines approaching the airfield from the town. Where could he go? Where could he hide?

Then he remembered the times he and his friends used to climb the cliff, daring each other to go higher. He crawled over the edge, broom still in hand. He couldn't leave it behind. He was maybe ten feet down when he heard the engines on the runway. They got closer, maybe halfway down the runway. Then the engines slowed, soon stopping. He heard voices, Pushtu voices. The Taliban. Ali had studied Pushtu in school. All Afghan schoolchildren first study only in their native language, Pushtu or Dari, depending on where they lived. In fourth grade, they begin studying the other language, in his case Pushtu. The voices were talking about where the plane was. It was soon evident they had not seen or heard a plane and were doubting whether it ever existed. They seemed to be mocking one of the group, whose voice spoke Pushtu with an accent like that of someone who didn't speak it fluently. After more questions, some cursing, and more muttering, the engines started up again, and the vehicles (it sounded like two) left. Ali waited a while, then peered cautiously over the edge onto the airfield. There was no one in sight. He decided to wait until it was dark to go anywhere. He stayed on the face of the cliff, eventually finding a small depression where he could hide from anyone above or below.

***

For a while, Ali felt sorry for himself. He wasn't going to see his family, and he was in great danger. He was hungry and thirsty, but he had no other place to go. On the other hand, his sister was nearby. She thought he had left to Iran, but he knew she would be overjoyed to see him. He could help her and protect her from the Taliban.

The imminent danger from the plane was no more, although the cloud of the Taliban still hung over Sharidure. While the Taliban were still around, he would be in danger. Maybe they would go away soon.

As it got darker, he climbed down to the river valley. He bent down to get a drink. Now, he was just hungry. Then he remembered his slingshot. He couldn't remember having to use it to hunt for food, having only hunted for fun.

The sight of two rabbits focused him on relieving his hunger. He stalked them and found his aim was as good as ever. He carried the rabbit back to the river to wash it. How could he cook it? Maybe the little building up on the airfield still had the matches and charcoal he and his friends used when they stayed there overnight. He was really hungry, so he walked around to the west side of the cliff, where it wasn't as steep and climbed back up to the runway. He peered cautiously into the darkness to see if possibly someone was watching the airfield. He couldn't see anyone, so he crawled up over the edge and walked as quietly as he could around the edge of the runway to the small building. He knew there was no light in it, but that was better anyway. He opened the door and found everything just as he remembered. In one corner was the box where they kept the matches and charcoal. To his great delight, matches and charcoal were still in the box. About an hour later, he was feasting on roast rabbit.

As for a place to go, he decided he would stay away from the town, but he could probably stay here. No one seemed to have been here for a long time. "That was enough for one day," he thought to himself. He would see what else to do in the morning. The walls protected him from the cool evening breeze, and he slept until morning.

***

He meant to wake up before sunrise, but when he got up and stretched, the light was seeping through the cracks around the door of the little building, his new home. He would have to wait another day, until dark, to go back to talk to Shireen. The Taliban might still be in Sharidure. When he opened the door and started out to return to the river for a drink, he saw someone coming up the path from town. He jumped back behind the building, hoping that someone did not see him. He waited, then lay down on the ground to take a peek around a corner of the building. It was a woman, not so surprising since there weren't any grown men in Sharidure. At first, he couldn't see who it was because her back was toward him. Then, she turned to go back down to town. It was Shireen! He wanted to call out, but someone else might be close by. He stepped slowly out from behind the building and softly called, "Shireen, it's me, Ali," then quickly added, "Don't say anything. Just walk over here." Shireen turned and gasped, then walked over to Ali.

"Ali, why are you here? Why didn't you leave?"

"I had to sweep out the tracks of the plane so the Taliban wouldn't know a plane was here. They did come; I heard them, but they didn't see me. They had someone with them, a Dari speaker, who must have told them the plane was here. I couldn't see or tell who it was. They went back down to the town." The words were tumbling out. "I stayed up here last night. I was afraid to come into town. Are the Taliban still here?"

"No, they left. But they said if a plane ever came, or if anyone came to help us, they would find out and come again. They said no one should have resisted them, reminding us of that awful day when they shot all the men."

Ali shuddered to think what might have happened if the Taliban had found the plane. "Shireen, it's not going to happen. Their time will come to leave. I don't think they want to live up here. They will lose interest and leave."

Shireen looked at him, and her tears dried up. She wiped her eyes, straightened up, even smiled, and added her own hope. "They can't hurt us any more than they have. All of my friends are determined to restore our town. We have a school for the children, we are growing wheat, and now we have started gardens. She looked down, not sure if she should tell Ali what else she wanted to say. "My brother, my greatest sorrow is that my husband was also killed by the Taliban. I watched him stand, tall and proud, facing the Taliban. He was the son of Askgar, the leader of our local Mujahudeen. His name was Ahmad Nabi."

"I knew him. He was part of the group that wrecked the Russian UAZs. He was a good person. I'm so sorry, Shireen."

"It's in the past. That time has gone. Now, we have to make a plan to get you back to Iran. The best way is by truck because the Taliban aren't so worried about people in trucks. They do search the buses. Ali, you have to leave today. There might be other informants around."

"But what about you? How will you survive?" Ali started to ask if she needed a man to help her, but he only thought it, then thought better of it. Maybe she could be all right by herself. He thought back about when they were growing up, and smiled at remembering when she fought some other kids when they made fun of his bent leg.

"What are you smiling about?"

"I was just thinking about how you fought those kids who were teasing me about my leg."

Shireen smiled, then laughed. "Those stupid girls. Some

of them are still here, and they're still stupid." They both laughed. It felt good to laugh.

"The trucks come in from Bamiyan in the afternoon and leave as soon as they can. They go from here over the Shahtoo pass to Pahnjwak. I'm sure they would give you a ride. There won't be any Taliban along the way until you get close to Herat. Make friends with the driver, and he'll hide and protect you. Maybe you can get all the way to the border. If a truck comes in, I'll come to get you, but for now, wait up here, and I'll bring you some tea and nawn." Shireen left to go get Ali something to eat. What she said made complete sense. Ali wasn't worried any more about his sister. He would make her safer by leaving, just as they discussed when they thought he would be leaving on the plane.

She came back soon with some hot tea, nawn, and even an egg. They talked about meeting again, though both wondered if that would ever come true. Ali told her more about his own new family and how they would love her and be a family for her. They talked about when they were young and the world was good and life was easy. "God willing, it will be good and easy again, Shireen Jahn." Ali was trying to give hope to his sister. She slowly walked back down to town to wait for a truck.

Chapter Twelve
Escape From the Taliban

That afternoon Shireen came back to get Ali. A truck was leaving soon for Pahnjwak. Brother and sister talked about what might lie ahead in their lives, as they walked down to Sharidure. Shireen gave Ali some nawn and apples for his trip. He climbed up into the back of the truck and waved, as the truck rumbled out of town. His last sight of his sister was her waving goodbye, as the truck rounded a curve in the road.

In Pahnjwak, there were no Taliban, just two more passengers. They were going to Jungal. When they arrived, late at night, the driver told Ali he might be able to stay in the weather station. It turned out to be empty, so no one objected to his staying. There were several rooms to choose from. The driver promised not to leave without him, but Ali got up as soon as it was light. He was grateful for the nawn and an apple Shireen gave him.

He found the truck parked outside a teahouse. The driver was just up and invited Ali to some hot tea. So far, his journey was as good as he could have hoped. That day, as the small towns went by, he and the driver talked about everything from the Taliban to the price of nawn to their schools. The driver was from Bamiyan. He told Ali about how the Taliban ruined the giant Buddhas and how it had saddened all of the people from Bamiyan. "No one can understand it. There was no reason. They were part of our ancestors, part of our hearts. It made everyone hate the Taliban even more. A fight is a fight, a war is a war, but the Buddhas were not part of this war."

Ali talked about his growing up in Sharidure and about his family in Muhshed. The driver told Ali he was only going as far as Herat, but he knew lots of drivers who made regular trips to Muhshed, and when they got to Heart, he found a truck leaving the next morning for Muhshed.

At the Iranian border the guards waved the truck through. They seemed to know the driver so Ali didn't even have to get down. They soon drove into Tyabad, where they had lunch. When Muhshed appeared on the horizon just before dark, Ali offered the driver money, but he waved Ali on and said he appreciated the company. Ali climbed down and waved as the truck pulled away. He was home again.

***

No one knew he was coming. He knocked on the door and waited. "Who is it?" It was Nafisa's voice.

"It's me, Ali. I'm home."

There was a running sound on the other side of the door. Nafisa, Hassan and Shireen all were there. Hassan and Shireen jumped up and down saying, "Baba, Baba! (Daddy, Daddy)" Ali and Nafisa hugged and were both almost knocked over by Hassan and Shireen.

"Are you tired? Would you like some tea? How about some aash? We just had some." Nafisa was so glad to have him home.

"Yes, to all of those. I haven't had anything like your aush since I left." Ali could picture Nafisa making the noodles and stirring the sour cream and vegetables to make the delicious soup.

"How did you get here? Reza told us about flying the plane out and how you had to sweep out the tracks. Did the Taliban come?"

"They did come, but not before I got all the tracks swept out. They came in two pickups, I think, though I didn't actually see them. I could only hear them. I was over the side of the cliff where they couldn't see me." Ali told them about the rest of the night, and the next days. He told them about his sister and about the journey in the truck to Muhshed. He didn't tell them about the continuing threat of the Taliban.

Hassan and Shireen wanted to have a story about Mullah Nasrudeen, the one about how Mullah Nasrudeen was the best chicken. Ali agreed but said they first had to tell him about their classes and what they were playing after school. They took turns sitting on his lap and telling him all about everything. It was great to be home.

***

About two months later, a stranger came into Sayeed's shop. He said he was from Bamiyan, and he was looking for someone from Sharidure named Ali. At first, Sayeed was suspicious of this stranger, but after further questioning, he decided that what he was saying was true, so he went to get Ali, who came to meet him. The man said that he was from Bamiyan, but that he had a sister living in Sharidure. He had come through there on his way to Muhshed to get cooking oil and kerosene. He had his own truck and made the trip every other month. His sister told him that she was a friend of Shireen and that Shireen was under suspicion of the Taliban. They thought she was teaching girls and were making life very difficult for her, threatening her, restricting where she went, watching her closely. She was afraid they might harm her more. The man said his sister thought Shireen had a brother in Iran, probably in Muhshed. He said he was a nephew of Akbar, Ali's father's friend, so he went there first to ask if there was someone from Sharidure who might be Shireen's brother. That's how he found Sayeed's shop. He knew the situation was very difficult for the people of Sharidure and wondered if he could bring something back to Shireen to help her survive.

Ali thanked him profusely, asked where he was staying in case he wanted to contact him, and went straight to his house to talk about what to do with Nafisa. "Ali, we have to help her. We are her only family. She must be so afraid. Do you think she could come here?"

"I don't think so. Women who aren't accompanied by a man from their household aren't allowed to go anywhere. Maybe we could send her some money. I trust this man from Bamiyan. He is a nephew of Akbar."

"Ali, what if you went to get her. Then she would be allowed to travel."

"Let's think about it tonight and decide in the morning. The man from Bamiyan isn't going back for several days because he has to get his truck loaded."

***

The morning was Friday, "Jumah," the holy day. There was no school, and the carpentry shop was closed. After morning prayers and the sermon by the mullah at the mosque, Ali and Nafisa sat back on the cushions in their home to decide what to do. They both wanted to do the best thing for their family but were worried about what might happen to Shireen, Ali's sister, if she stayed in Sharidure. They finally decided that Ali had to go back to convince her to come to Iran. When they talked it over with Nafisa's family, they agreed they couldn't just leave Ali's sister alone, so it was decided.

If the Taliban were suspicious of why Ali was there, he was going to say he was a teacher and wanted to start a school for boys. Shireen helped him gather several levels of teacher books. He also started letting his beard grow to help him be accepted by the Taliban. His own children thought it strange to see him with a beard. They had never seen him with one.

The truck was to leave on Monday for Bamiyan. The driver agreed to have Ali ride along. He was glad to do his part to help. There were lots of hugs and tears, but everyone was prepared for the separation. It would be a short one, probably not more than a couple of weeks. The truck driver assured them he would continue making the trip so Ali and Shireen were assured of a way back to Iran. It was a good plan. Even Ali's beard was cooperating, coming in dark and thick.

Again the border crossing was uneventful. The evening of the second day saw the truck rumbling into the outskirts of Sharidure. Ali invited the driver to stay for the night. He was glad to accept, after turning down the initial offer. That was only polite.

Shireen was totally surprised to see Ali when she greeted him at the door of their home. After a warm meal, the driver took his things to the carpentry shop and parked his truck in front.

Ali told Shireen of the plan. She liked the part about him being a teacher but insisted she could not leave because the girls needed her as their teacher. She was having small groups attending sewing lessons, and secretly teaching them to read, write, and learn mathematics.

In the morning, a Taliban representative was at the door, asking who Ali was and why he was here. Ali told him he was Shireen's brother, that he was here to be a teacher for boys, and he just returned from Iran. The Taliban representative asked for some proof, so Ali showed him the teacher books he had. That seemed to impress him. He left making a

Inside Boys' School • By Howard Faber

comment about Ali's fledgling beard, but also saying it was

good that he was trying to grow a beard in accordance with Taliban requirements.

So it was, that Ali became the official teacher of the boys of Sharidure.

It worked out really well. It was completely out in the open. He had a reason to be there. It was also a big relief for Shireen because she could now leave her home, accompanied by her brother, an adult male, thus appropriate to the Taliban regulations.

However, it was a change in the plans for Ali. They would not be leaving as soon as he expected. He would have to let his family in Muhshed know.

***

"Shireen, I overheard two of the Taliban talking today. They were saying they have heard rumors of a secret school for girls. They said they are going to search all of the houses until they find it. You have to stop." This was one of Shireen's friends. She had come to Shireen and Ali's house this morning to warn them. Shireen immediately went to tell Ali what her friend said. Maybe one of the children had somehow been overheard or one of the families. That night, Shireen only had sewing classes, no school. When the girls asked why, she told them she was waiting for new books, so they would have to wait to have more classes until the books came.

The next morning, Ali found one of the dreaded night letters on the outside of their door. It said they were suspected of having classes for girls, and unless the lessons stopped, their home would be burned, and they would be punished. He didn't tell Shireen but he was very worried. They would have to leave.

Where could they go? Should he tell Shireen? He decided he would have to tell her, and they would both have to go. He couldn't leave her by herself. He also knew they would be closely watched.

"Shireen, the Taliban suspect us of holding classes for girls. They will now be watching us carefully." He didn't tell her about the night letter. "I think we should leave secretly but not right away. We have to think up a way to make it seem not to be suspicious when we leave."

Shireen could tell that this was a serious matter. She was afraid. "Ali, maybe this is the time for us to leave. Do you have any ideas about where to go?"

"No, I'm hesitant to try to stay with people we know. It would put them in danger. We also have to make the Taliban think we aren't acting strange. We have to let them see us do our normal things, like having school for the boys, getting water, going shopping, all of the usual things."

"I think that's right, but we should also plan our escape."

They went ahead with classes for the boys that day. That afternoon Shireen went with Ali to the homes of the girls that were attending sewing classes to tell the families there would be no more lessons until further notice.

They also started the plan for their escape. They walked to the eastern end of town, to the bridge over the irrigation canal, down the other side of the canal, to the river in the valley. They collected some driftwood from the river and carried it back to their home. They made sure anyone watching saw them do this. They repeated this every day for a week, establishing a routine that became part of their normal activities. Every evening, they carried with them picnic supplies, blankets to sit on, and even a small grill for cooking.

***

When Naeem, the driver from Bamiyan, came through with his truck, heading west to Iran, Ali invited him into the carpentry shop to see if he would help them. Ali asked if he could take the other route to Jungal, following the river west. That way they could bypass Pahnjwak and several other small towns on the road to Jungal. Ali explained that he and his sister had to leave secretly. They would meet him at sunrise tomorrow morning along the river on the way to Jungal. Without asking lots of questions, Naeem agreed, but said he couldn't wait long for them, as he had to be halfway to Iran the next night.

The time came for them to leave, and that evening they packed up their usual picnic supplies and headed east of town to the riverbed to have their usual picnic. They turned for a last look at their home. It would be the last time they saw it.

On the way to the bridge, they walked past several Taliban. They tried their best to look like it was the same as every other time. No one stopped them as they went down to the river. Today, unlike before, they walked further along the river, following it back west, until they were out of sight of town. They worried that someone would notice, but no one did.

It was a long night, cold after the sun went down. They wrapped up in the blankets, waiting by the river on the way toward Jungal. They talked for a while, about their parents, about Ali's new family, about growing up. They didn't talk about what might happen if they were discovered.

Just after sunrise, they heard the sound of a truck approaching. At first, they hid, unsure of whether it was the truck from Bamiyan. When they could see that it was, they stood up and waved for the driver to stop. He climbed down quickly from the cab, looking back toward town to be sure he had not been followed. He apologized, but asked them to sit in the back of the truck, inside a box he made and hid under his cargo. Inside were two quilts to soften the ride. It was not the most comfortable of places, but they both realized that he was trying to help them and hide them from anyone asking questions. The truck rumbled away, following the river west. That afternoon when they pulled into Jungal, the precautions proved very wise. Several Taliban were stopping each vehicle entering the town. Ali and Shireen could hear the Pushtu speakers asking Naeem if he had seen a man and woman on the road into town. He could truthfully say he hadn't. They asked if he had seen anyone like that in Pahnjwak. Again, he could truthfully say he hadn't. Ali and Shireen then heard someone climbing up on the back of the truck to look at what was on board. Their hearts beat faster. Surely, they would be discovered.

The footsteps didn't climb down into the truck bed, but instead climbed back down to the ground. Naeem was also sweating, trying not to let anyone see. He went into a teahouse and took his time having tea and ordering nawn. He thought about ordering extra but decided against it for fear of raising suspicion about taking some along.

Shireen and Ali kept completely quiet, waiting, waiting. At last, they heard Naeem climb back into the cab, start the truck, and shift into gear. The truck began its journey further west. They spent the rest of the day and the next night inside their cozy box. They weren't so much cold as hungry and thirsty, but, they and the truck driver realized he couldn't take the chance of anyone seeing him going back to bring them anything. Finally, about noon of the next day, Naeem stopped between towns, looked back and ahead down the road, and climbed into the back to bring them some nawn and tea. They talked briefly. He said they would be in Iran after dark that evening. He was still worried about the border. He hoped the border guards on the Afghan side would be the usual guards he knew and saw on his trips. Eventually, Ali and Shireen slept.

They woke when the bumping of the truck stopped. They could hear someone talking, though they couldn't make out what was said. They waited for the sound of someone climbing up the back of the truck. It never came. The truck started out again, then stopped again in a short time. This time the talking was closer. Apparently the driver had not stepped down. Ali recognized the Iranian accent of the speaker. They were in Iran!

***

When Ali knocked on his door that night in Muhshed, Shireen wasn't sure how she was feeling. She was worried about being accepted by Ali's family. She felt like she was the cause of him being separated from them for so long. She also felt like an intruder; she had never met his wife or children. Maybe they wouldn't be able to understand her because of the difference in Iranian and Afghan Farsi. She also knew she wasn't looking her best, having ridden in the back of a truck for two days. She must look a mess.

Her fears were alleviated when the door opened to silhouette three surprised but joyous greeters. After hugging Ali, they turned their attention to Shireen. Ali introduced each. "Shireen, this is my wonderful wife, Nafisa."

"Welcome to our home. We have been hoping you could come. You must be very tired. Come in. Let's have some tea and talk." This was Nafisa putting the doubts of Shireen about being welcome to rest.

"Shireen, this is my son Hassan. Don't you think he looks a lot like dad?"

Hassan was smiling. "Dad told us about you. I know you're a teacher. Could you help me with my homework?" Shireen smiled and nodded.

"And, Shireen, this is Shireen."

"Aunt Shireen, I've been waiting a long time to say that. You're my very first aunt."

Now Shireen (aunt Shireen) was crying. She had been alone for such a long time. "I'm sorry. I didn't mean to cry.

I'm not sad. Ali, Nafisa, Hassan, and Shireen, thank you, thank you for bringing me into your home."

They had some green tea, some aush, some cookies, and lots of talk and laughter. Ali was home with his family, and Shireen was safe. Sharidure seemed far away.

Chapter Thirteen
Americans in Afghanistan and Ali
Brings His Family Back Home

That fall they heard on the radio the news of the Americans arriving in Afghanistan. The men of the Northern Alliance and the Americans swept toward Kabul. They didn't hear any news about Bamiyan and whether the Taliban were still there. It was Naeem, the truck driver, who told them about the Taliban fleeing back to Pakistan. Bamiyan and Sharidure were free of them. People were playing music and flying kites. Life was returning to normal in the Hazarajat.

"Did you see our home in Sharidure?"

"Not really. The town seemed quiet and I didn't see a lot of destruction. I think the Taliban left in a hurry. I only stopped at the teahouse for lunch."

That evening Ali and Shireen began to plan their return

to their faraway home.

***

At first, Shireen insisted she should go with Ali. "It's my home, too. The girls will need a teacher."

"Shireen, let me go first to be sure it's safe. There still might be Taliban around. If it is safe, I'll let you know, and you can come. It would also make me feel better about leaving Nafisa here with our children. You could be a big help to her."

In the end, they agreed that Ali should go to see what exactly the situation was in Sharidure and Shireen would stay in Muhshed to help Nafisa with the home, possibly even teach to earn money for the family. When Ali went to tell Nafisa about the plan, she was the first to speak. "Ali, I know you need to go back to Sharidure. Don't worry about us. My family is here to help us."

Ali was so relieved to hear her say this. He told her about what he and Shireen planned, and Nafisa was pleased that Shireen was going to stay. She told him how much she would miss him. She didn't say anything about what they would do if Sharidure was safe and whether they would go there to live.

When Ali left that morning with Naeem in the truck

back to Afghanistan, it was a sad farewell to his children. They cried and asked when he would be back. "You know about how the snow comes in the winter. I promise to be back before it gets here. Your job is to learn everything you can in school and to take care of your mom and aunt Shireen. I think I can send you letters again. I'll be back soon."

When they got to the Afghan-Iranian border, the change was noticeable. There was no one there. There were no Taliban checking the trucks. Ali's hopes grew as they went east, toward Sharidure. When they came around the last curve in the road into Sharidure, Ali couldn't wait to get back to his home, maybe for the final time. He was thinking about what to do first. The truck stopped at the teahouse, where he saw several familiar faces, and no bearded black-turbaned Taliban. The people there greeted him warmly. They asked about his family. He asked about their family. "Are you well? Your family?"

"Fine, we're all well."

He didn't ask about the Taliban.

He left the teahouse and said goodbye to Naeem, the truck driver. "Thank you very much. May peace be with you."

Ali walked toward his home. When he got there, it was only a pile of broken bricks and wooden beams. Even the compound walls had been smashed. There was nothing left of his home. He could guess what happened. When the Taliban couldn't find Shireen and him, they must have been very angry, so they took it out on their home. He walked around, looking for their well and garden. Thankfully, they hadn't destroyed either. Tomorrow, he would start to rebuild his home. For tonight, he could sleep in his father's shop, if it was still standing.

It was. Maybe the Taliban hadn't realized it belonged to his family. Maybe they did and were watching it to see if he would come back, so he stopped across the street and looked carefully at the shop. There was no sign of anyone in or around the shop. He climbed up on a rooftop to see the whole area better. He lay down, so no one on the street would see him on the roof. There were no black-bearded men with turbans that he could see. He decided to quietly walk by a back street to the government building to see if there were Taliban guards there. The open area in front of the building was empty. Usually there would have been children playing, rolling hoops or playing games. Tonight, it was only still, only empty, only quiet. He thought of the times he and his friends played there. That seemed long ago. He decided to spend the night at the airfield, in the little shed he helped build. In the morning, he would look again for the Taliban.

He slept fitfully, his sleep full of dreams, or maybe just thoughts of what had been in Sharidure. The morning sun lit up the frame around the door to the shed. Ali sat up, stretched, yawned, then stood up to walk down to the town below. He took a back route, avoiding any people who might be up and about. The Taliban were a worry. He watched the streets from above the town, seeing people leave their homes, seeing a town awaken, seeing the teahouse open, the street in front of it sprinkled with water, then swept, owposhee. There were no signs of any Taliban, so he decided they were no longer there.

Ali spent that first morning in the shop. Several people stopped by, welcoming him back, asking about his family. One asked if he would be doing carpentry. He decided he would, needing money to live. He brought some from Iran, but if he intended to stay, he would need a way to live.

The teahouse was open, so he went there for lunch. There was some talk of the Taliban, but no one had seen them. Was it possible they were gone? After lunch, he went again to his home, now destroyed. To bring his family, he would have to rebuild it and he started to do just that. He laid out the outlines, using stones to mark the outside walls, then went back to the shop to begin the frame. He decided to build his new home a little bigger than the old one. His new family was larger than the one he grew up in. Shireen would need a bedroom and perhaps a study for her books, with a table to use to do her homework from school. Surely, she would want to teach again. Someone at the teahouse asked about that. It was a good feeling to be planning his family's future. It was also good to be working.

He sent a letter with Naeem, the truck driver from Bamiyan, when the truck came through on its way to Iran. He told Nafisa about the shop and how he was rebuilding the home. He even asked her about how to design the house. Naeem would be back next week with a letter in return. Meanwhile, he kept an eye out for Taliban. No one had seen them for a week. A normal life was slowly returning to

Sharidure. Children were playing with hoops, flying kites, and even talking about school.

When the letter from Nafisa came on the truck, Ali's hopes got even higher. She asked him when he wanted her and the children to come to Sharidure. He worked late on the house that night. Several people asked if they could help. After a week, the compound walls were up. After two weeks, the walls of the house were finished. After three weeks, the roof was on. He started on the inside walls, following Nafisa's wishes. He ordered glass for the windows from Bamiyan. Naeem brought them, wrapped carefully in cloth and cotton. Ali set the window glass into the frames he built, and he started living in the house. He carefully wrote about the new home to Nafisa and asked if she and the children could come see it. When her letter came back, she told him that she and their children, Shireen his sister, and her father would come on the next trip Naeem made from Muhshed to Sharidure.

***

The next three years were like heaven. Ali had his family back with him. Nafisa and Shireen restarted a school for the children of Sharidure. Ali and his father-in-law made

Oxen Team • By Rex Blumhagen

the carpentry shop the biggest business in town. There were many things to be rebuilt. Other families came back to restart their family businesses. The farmers had good crops.

The winters weren't too severe, but there was enough snow to make the rivers run and let Ali teach Shireen and Hassan the joys of sliding down hills on sleds he made.

There was a new governor in Bamiyan, Afghanistan's first woman governor. She wanted schools and electricity for Bamiyan's people. One of the roads from Kabul was being hard-surfaced. Even the Buddhas the Taliban destroyed were getting attention, as there were plans to restore them. A hotel and restaurant were built to make tourists feel they could again come to Bamiyan. There was even talk of an ancient reclining Buddha somewhere in the Bamiyan valley. There had always been stories about this giant Buddha that disappeared.

There was, however, talk of the Taliban gaining footholds not so far away in Wardak and Oruzgon. The Kabul government wanted all the provinces to give up their weapons, so there could not again be militias to fight for control of Afghanistan.

***

At the carpentry shop Ali told Nafisa's father, Sayeed, about what he heard that morning. "The Taliban are stopping trucks on the road from Wardak. They demand money and take what they want from the trucks. That road comes into Bamiyan over a pass. My guess is that they will try to again take over Bamiyan."

"Are these people likely to get into Bamiyan?"

"Some of the men have been saying we have to again get weapons to defend ourselves, because the government may not be able to protect us. I have been meeting with some of the men of Sharidure to plan how to protect us if we have to.

My father was killed by the Taliban. I ran from them when I was younger, but I won't run away again. This is my home. We have all agreed to fight if we have to. Before, when the Taliban were in control of most of Afghanistan, the last two places they didn't have control were the Panjsheer and the Hazarajat. They never did get control of the Panjsheer and the only reason they took over here was the help they got from Pakistan. It will be much harder for Pakistan to directly help them now. The Americans and Europeans will keep them from doing that up here, but we need weapons to protect ourselves from the Taliban in Wardak and Oruzgon. The people there don't have any way to protect themselves, and the Afghan army and police aren't able to."

"How many men are there to fight?"

"We are twenty-six."

"You now have twenty-seven. Do you have weapons?"

"We have eight automatic rifles we took from the Russians when we dropped them into the irrigation canal. We also have two machine guns that were on the UAVs."

Sayeed looked at his son-in-law with new respect. Ali never mentioned this. "Is there any way to get more weapons?"

Ali and his friends had been talking about this. "The government won't give us any. We think the best way is to take them from the Taliban. We know from the truck drivers where they stop the trucks, and we have a plan about ambushing them and taking weapons. We have to do it quietly, so the government doesn't hear about it."

"How many Taliban are stopping the trucks?"

"There have been usually eight or ten." Ali was talking softly now.

"One raid wouldn't be enough to get rifles for all of the men."

"We plan to make two raids. We plan to capture the first group of Taliban so they can't go back to report about what happened, but we want the second group to go back to report so the Taliban know it won't be so easy to retake Bamiyan."

Sayeed was beginning to respect his son-in-law even more.

Chapter Fourteen
Raiding the Taliban

They decided to have eight men go on the first raid. The main reason was there were just eight weapons. The plan was to go to one of the places on the road where the Taliban were stopping trucks, wait for a truck to pass and be stopped, then let the truck go, and surround the Taliban when they were celebrating. The hard part would be staying hidden from the Taliban and still be able to surround them. Ali thought the Taliban would not expect any attacks, so they would be surprised and not ready to fight back.

They left at dusk, each leaving from a separate place so as not to attract attention. They met outside of town and followed paths used by the nomads when they visited in the summer. Ali had not told Nafisa or the children. Only Nafisa's father knew, and even he did not know details of the plan. They walked silently, moving above the road, each thinking his own thoughts. Ali grew more determined as he walked. He would not leave again. He would defend his home and family.

As they approached the place they thought the Taliban would wait for trucks, they split into two groups, one for each side of the road. Soon they heard Pushtu. The Taliban were very sure of themselves, expecting no resistance. Ali and the men from Sharidure waited to figure out how many Taliban there were and where they were. From the voices, there seemed to be seven. By now it was dark. Soon, they heard the sound of a truck laboring with its load up the pass. They moved closer. The engine sounded louder, and the headlights spread their circles of light on the road. They moved closer and they could see the Taliban crouching by the road.

As the truck appeared around a turn, four of the Taliban moved onto the road ahead of the truck, brandishing their weapons. The truck came to a stop and the driver appeared, hands raised, pleading for his life. The Taliban laughed, then motioned the two passengers to step down. Three more Taliban appeared at the back of the truck, looking for the driver's assistant who rode there.

The Taliban weren't interested in killing the people. They wanted money and supplies. One of the things on the truck was a shipment of kharbooza, the wonderful melons grown in the north. They were one of the things the Taliban took. The truck soon left with its relieved passengers. The Taliban gathered on the road, laughing about how easy it had been. They soon cut open one of the melons, then sat down to eat.

When Ali saw them put down their rifles, he ran out from where he was hiding, shouting in Pushtu for the Taliban to stay sitting and not to pick up their rifles. The other Sharidure men swiftly joined him, surrounding the Taliban. Two of the Taliban reached for their rifles and four shots rang out. Both Taliban fell to the ground screaming, clutching their legs where they had been hit. Ali told his men to aim low so the Taliban couldn't duck under their fire, and because they wanted to keep the Taliban alive. The other Taliban stayed seated, eyeing their attackers. The Taliban weapons were quickly moved out of their reach. The bandoliers of bullets worn by the Taliban were removed and were soon on the shoulders of the men from Sharidure. Two Taliban were ordered to carry the two wounded men.

The rest of the night was spent marching the prisoners to an abandoned sheep and goat corral where families used

Stone Corral • By Howard Faber

to live in the summer. At the base of the stone corral, there were small holes dug horizontally into the ground. The Sharidure men put one Taliban into each hole and rolled a large stone into the small opening.

They put some water and a little food into each hole. As each hole was secured, Ali told each of the Taliban they would be kept here for several days. They would be allowed to live to return to their homes. He also told them he and his friends wanted to live peacefully in their homes, but that they would be fighting anyone who tried to attack them. They left two men to guard the corral.

The others got back to Sharidure before sunrise. No one missed them. Ali explained to Nafisa that he had been on a night training mission to help defend the village.

That night the twenty-five men from Sharidure met to discuss what to do next. The seven Taliban weapons and extra ammunition were given out into eager hands.

***

There was a debate going on about what to do with the Taliban prisoners. Some wanted to kill them. Some wanted to let them go. Some wanted to turn them over to Afghan authorities. In the end, it was decided that it was wise to return them to the road where they were captured, so they could find their way home. There was also discussion about telling them where their captors were from. So far, only Ali had spoken to them, and only in Pushtu. The location of the deserted corral also gave no clue as to where they were or what town was the home of their captors. It was decided to keep up this veil of secrecy. It would be good to keep the Taliban from reprisal raids.

Ali went with six others to relieve the current rotation of guards. There had been eight hour shifts for the guards. He brought with him clean cloth to replace the temporary bandages they had used to stop the bleeding from the legs of the wounded Taliban.

On the third night after the raid, the Taliban prisoners were removed from their silent little prisons. They blinked and rubbed their eyes and mumbled to each other about their ordeal. Ali led them back to where the truck was stopped. He told them they could find their way home from there, but not to return. "This is our home. Go back to yours, and leave us alone. You can see we are ready for you if you come back. Next time, we will aim higher. Oh, and thank you for your rifles."

Ali and the other men returned to Sharidure and made plans for a second raid. They wanted to send a signal to the Taliban who were stopping trucks approaching their town from the west. They also needed more weapons and bullets. The raid was planned for the next night. The strategy was the same as the first raid. This time they took ten men since they had more weapons.

They walked in silence, again following animal paths above the main road, stopping at the location they heard was where Taliban ambushes took place. They were more confident than the first time, but this time they had a longer wait.

Finally, in the morning, a truck came growling up from the west. They saw it stop, with Taliban fighters surrounding it. There were nine in this group. As before, they let down their guard when the truck rumbled off. Then an argument started about dividing up the money they had taken. The argument turned into a fight. They were so focused on the dispute that they didn't notice Ali and the Sharidure men coming from both sides of the road. Only when it was too late and they were surrounded did they notice the new arrivals. Ali told them to sit with their hands above their heads. He thanked them for their rifles. Three of the Sharidure men collected the Taliban bullet bandoliers. Another relieved them of the money taken from the truck. "We have a convenient hotel for you for the next couple of days." They were marched to the same corral used by the first captive group.

When Ali and seven of the other men returned to Sharidure they were greeted by a group of American soldiers who arrived that morning. They wanted to talk to the leaders of the village.

"We would like to help you defend your village." Ali and

his father-in-law were completely surprised at the words of the American leader. They exchanged glances, both wondering if they should tell this outsider about their now functioning fighting group. They asked the American for a little time to talk about his offer.

"I don't trust this outsider." These were Ali's father-in-law's first words. "What does he know of our situation?

Remember how the Russians said they were going to help us."

Now it was Ali's turn. He wanted to be respectful of his

American Soldier • UNO

father-in-law. "I do remember the Russians and the Taliban, but we could use some help. These are the Americans, not the Russians."

There was silence.

"So you think we should talk more to them? Should we tell them about our group?" Sayeed seemed to be warming a little to the idea of help.

"What does it hurt to talk? We should first ask more about how they could help and try to find out if they are really Americans."

They went back outside to talk more to the Americans. Ali started to realize that his village was assuming he was the leader, and he warmed to the idea and the accompanying responsibility. He invited the entire group into his carpentry shop to have tea. Sayeed and the other people standing with them nodded their heads in agreement with that invitation. It was polite and proper to invite outsiders to tea.

The Americans talked among themselves about having tea. They recognized it was polite and proper. Ali wished he knew English because he couldn't understand what was being said. With the Americans was an Afghan. Ali judged him to be Tajik, apparently a translator. The American leader spoke some Farsi, with a definite accent. So far the translator had not spoken to the people of Sharidure.

There were no chairs in Ali's shop, and everyone stood. The Americans seemed fine with standing, but the Afghans were used to sitting. Ali thought of a compromise. He quickly made a circular space in the shop and swept the floor. He asked his son Hassan, who was close by watching and listening, to bring the cushions from their home. "How many leeoff do we have Hassan?"

"I think we have six, father." Hassan ran home and soon returned, loaded down with cushions and helped by two of his friends. Ali placed the long cushions in a circle, knelt down and gestured for the Americans to join him and the other Afghans. The tea arrived from the teashop. The shop windows were full of faces, everyone wanting to see these outsiders and what was going on.

"Thank you very much," the American leader said, as he realized the importance of this first meeting. "We have come from Bamiyan. Before that we were at the American base at Bagram. My leader asked us to go to your village to help you protect yourselves. We stopped at Bamiyan to get permission from your governor to help. She thinks it's a good idea. I have a letter from her to you."

He handed a letter to Ali, who read the letter. It verified that these soldiers were indeed Americans, and that their help was approved by her and the government of Afghanistan. It recommended allowing the Americans to help them defend their town. The letter went on to say that the Americans might stay a month or more to train the village men to protect themselves, but then they would move on to another village. Ali explained this to Sayeed and the other village people. Ali and the other village leaders stood to leave and talk further about the offer of help. He explained to the Americans (through their translator) that he would be back after discussing it with the other village leaders. He told the Americans they could stay in the shop until he returned and to enjoy the tea and nawn that would be coming.

The men of Sharidure went to the school to talk about what to do. Most of them were in favor of accepting the help. Some were fearful of reprisals from Taliban if it became known Americans were there.

Ali waited until everyone had spoken. "When the Taliban last came to our town they left a bitter memory for our people. Perhaps all of you had a father or uncle killed that day. They are trying to come here again. Stopping trucks at the passes is just their first step. I left my home once. I will not leave again. The Americans can help us prepare for the day the Taliban come again."

There was a long silence. The men of Sharidure looked at each other, nodded, then stood. It was agreed. They would all prepare to defend their homes, and the Americans could help.

They returned to the carpentry shop to tell the Americans of their decision. Ali invited the soldiers to stay for the night, and they would talk more in the morning.

When Ali returned to his house, he found Nafisa, his sister Shireen, and his children all eager to know more about the Americans. He explained to his family about what was decided. They had many questions he couldn't answer, and they seemed glad to have help.

***

"My name is Ali. The people have asked me to speak to you about your help."

"I am Colonel Elliot." The American leader knew some Farsi. He turned to his translator and asked him to explain how they could help the people of Sharidure.

"Ali, my name is Ahmroodeen. I have been training with this group of Americans for three months. Colonel Elliot is a good man. We can help you. We didn't tell you, but last night, we had guards posted to warn of any danger."

This would be the first of several surprises to the Americans. "Yes, I know. Our guards were protecting your guards." Ali smiled as he said this and he smiled even more when he saw the reactions of Ahmroodeen and Colonel Elliot.

"How many guards did you have out?" asked Colonel Elliot.

Ali thought he noticed a tone of respect from both. "We have three posts. We rotate men every four hours. I'm sorry we don't have more. We are also covering another post."

"How many men do you have at a post?" Colonel Elliot was doing a quick calculation and wanted to know more about Ali and his men.

"Just one. We don't have very many men."

"So that's eight in an eight hour period. Are they on guard during the daytime, too?"

"Yes."

"So that's twenty-four in a full day. So you have at least twenty-four men?"

"Yes." Ali was thinking about the fact that they had only twenty-four rifles. That was another reason they had just one person on a shift at each post. He wasn't ready to tell that to the American.

"You mentioned another post. Is it overlooking your town? I know you have three roads into Sharidure . That's where we posted our guards, but you already know where we had our guards." He said the last sentence with a chuckle.

When he heard the translation from Ahmroodeen, it was Ali's turn to smile. He was beginning to like this outsider. He was also ready to share some new information. "We are guarding some Taliban prisoners we captured in a raid the night before you came. They are in a hotel some distance away from here."

Now, the colonel and the translator were really surprised and gaining more respect by the minute for these supposedly untrained, unarmed, simple townspeople. "We might have a few things to learn from the people of Sharidure."

Ali went on to explain how they had captured the Taliban in the night raid. He also told them about the first raid and how they sent that group back where they came from. The colonel had many questions about their strategy, how many men they used, how they knew where to attack. He nodded his head in approval at each part of the plan.

Ali asked him what he thought they should do with the Taliban. He explained to the colonel the Sharidure fighters thought they should release them like they had the first group. He went on to explain their thinking, that they wanted the Taliban to know they were not going to be able to take over Sharidure again, and they were ready to fight. They also wanted the Taliban to go back to their homes, and they were welcome to stay in the Pushtu speaking area because that was their home. The people from Sharidure were not interested in taking someone else's home from them or trying to tell them how to live.

"My father, Hassan, was killed by Taliban in Sharidure. He was lined up along with the other men and shot. My mother and sister were forced to watch. I already left for Iran, or I would have been killed, too."

Colonel Elliot listened intently to Ali. He learned a lot in a short time about this village and especially about one of its sons.

***

As they walked to the "hotel" for the Taliban, following

animal paths through the hills, Colonel Elliot, through Ahmroodeen the translator, told Ali about what an agreement between Sharidure and the Americans included. Now it was time for Ali to be surprised. A new school would be built, including all new books and desks for the children. The school would include a small hospital staffed initially by one of the Americans. The colonel introduced him to Ali. He knew enough to say in Farsi, "Hello, my name is Dr. Bettinga. I have with me medicine and other medical supplies. I will be taking care of the soldiers and your people."

Immediately Ali thought of the doctors who lived in Sharidure when he was little. What were their names? Hagel. Yes, that was it, Dr. Hagel and Dr. Hagel. He reached down to his knee, so magically repaired by them. He used to carry a crutch. Now, he carried an automatic rifle. There used to be a hospital in Sharidure and he was beginning to think there would be one again. Perhaps, the hospital could be a separate building, maybe even stand where the old one that was smashed by the Taliban used to stand.

As they came closer to the corral where the Taliban were kept, Ali asked again what the colonel thought should be done with them. His answer surprised both Ali and the translator. "I think your idea is a good one. They need to know you can and will fight back if they return. They will be bound to respect you more than they did before. If we take them back to the Bagram Air Base we will have to take care of them. I doubt any of them are high ranking commanders, so any information we could get from them would be not very new or useful. I think we should stay out of sight and let you deal with them."

Ali nodded his head in agreement. He motioned everyone to be silent and pointed to a position where the Americans could watch but not be seen. He gave the agreed on greeting for the villager on guard. He pointed to where the Americans were hiding and whispered some directions about what to do next, then rolled back the stones securing the Taliban in their little sleeping places. They crawled out and stood blinking in the daylight. He spoke only in Pushtu. He and the four villagers who came along held their rifles on the Taliban as Ali told them what was going to happen. "We will take you back to where you stopped the truck. If you do not try to escape or resist us, we will not harm you. If you do try to resist or escape, you will be shot."

One of the men from Sharidure led the way back to the place where they captured the Taliban. The Americans followed at a distance, far enough away that the Taliban were not aware of their presence. When they got to that place on the road west of Sharidure, Ali told them to stop and asked if they knew how to get back home from there.

They said they did. The one who seemed to be their leader added, "We will be back to take over again like we did before. We know what's best for you simple people. We know what you look like and we promise to come back to find you."

Ali's reply rang out in the sunlit afternoon. "This is our home. You do not belong here. We will fight for our home, just as you would fight for yours. We do not want your land or to tell you how to live. Go back to your homes and families. Leave us alone!"

The men from Sharidure watched as the Taliban headed down the road, west, away from Sharidure. When they were out of sight, Ali and his men headed east, back home, joined by the Americans.

Chapter Fifteen
Taliban Attack Sharidure

That night, it was Ali's turn to be on guard from midnight until four a.m. As he left his warm home, he glanced back to see one of the other Sharidure men heading the other way to take his turn on guard. Ali climbed up the hill above town, stopping on the level area where the nomads used to set up their tents as they passed through. He looked down on the sleeping village, where he could see his home where Nafisa, Shireen his sister, and Shireen and Hassan, his children, were all asleep. He smiled, turned, and climbed higher to the place where he would relieve the man currently on guard. They exchanged silent signals that all was well. The other man disappeared down the hill toward town.

About an hour later, Ali thought he heard someone speaking. The quiet words were in Pushtu. He crawled silently toward the sounds. Now he could make out the words. "Should we put it in the school or the teahouse?"

"A second voice replied, "The school. It will kill more of them."

The voices, it sounded like at least three, started down the hill towards Sharidure. Ali checked his rifle and picked out a path that would be steeper but get him close to where the voices were headed. The voices stopped. All he could hear was the sound of his own breathing. Then, he heard someone headed straight toward him and someone moving off to one side of him. They heard him and were splitting up to surround him. The approaching footsteps slowed, then stopped. Maybe they weren't sure where he was or even if there was someone there. He decided to move toward a group of large boulders to his left. They would provide some protection. As he crept toward the boulders, he realized he had to alert the other guards and Colonel Elliot and the soldiers. He needed help. "If I fire my rifle, my friends will be alerted, but I will also give away my position." His mind raced to come up with the best plan.

The fact that the intruders split up could work to his

advantage. He decided to attack one of them, move, then wait to find another one. As he crawled toward where he last heard footsteps, the moon went behind some clouds. As it disappeared, he saw the turbaned, bearded outline of a man standing next to a boulder. This was not someone from Sharidure.

He crept closer, got to his feet, crouched, them leapt at the figure. The collision sent both men to the ground. The whoosh of air from the surprised intruder's lungs changed to a groan, then a shout. No doubt his fellow intruders would be on their way. Ali scrambled to his feet, found the trigger on his rifle, and fired. The sound of the shot echoed on the hillside, and was followed by a scream of pain. Ali quickly moved away, found a large rock, and waited. Below in his town, the flickering light of kerosene lanterns appeared. The sound of the shot had been heard and help would be on the way.

"Go ahead, and carry out our mission. I'll take care of this Hazara dog." Ali heard this and shivered. He had to try to get the bomber, before he could place the bomb in Sharidure. He moved to his left. That was a good move because a burst of bullets splattered the rock where he had been sitting. He couldn't tell where the shots came from, so he kept moving, heading toward another group of boulders. More shots were fired, and these kicked up dust behind him. They came from his left. He dove behind a rock. More rounds bounced off the rock in front of him.

"Hurry up." The other guards must be getting closer.

They were. A burst of rounds came from behind him toward where his attacker was. Now, the odds were getting better, but he had to be careful about hitting or being hit by his own friends. Then there was another burst of bullets, this time from the Taliban attacker toward the second Sharidure guard. Ali had seen exactly where those rounds came from, and as it turned out, so had the third Sharidure guard. There was another burst of bullets, followed by a scream, then some wild firing into the air. The attacker was hit. The three Sharidure men closed in. They moved in cautiously and found their attacker slumped against a rock, his rifle on the ground, mumbling, wheezing. He was no longer a danger to them or to Sharidure.

***

By now there were many men and boys from Sharidure up above town where Ali intercepted the would-be attackers. The townspeople were curious about who they were. The word Taliban was the most common answer. Colonel Elliot and several of his men arrived just after the Sharidure guards. His men quickly carried the two wounded attackers away. Neither could walk. One was unconscious.

"Were there more?" Colonel Elliot and Ahmroodeen walked with Ali back down to town.

"There were at least three. I didn't see the other one, but I heard three voices." Ali did not add what he heard the last two say, about carrying out their mission and placing it in the school. It was beginning to get light.

"I'll have my men search this hill. Could your men search the village?"

Ali nodded in agreement. His men knew the village, and the Americans didn't. The men from Sharidure also knew the people, who belonged and who didn't.

After about an hour, the American soldiers returned from searching the hills above town. No one had been found. When they came back to town, Colonel Elliot came to talk to

Ali. No one had yet been found in town who didn't belong. It was then that Ali told Colonel Elliot about the plans he overheard. It was decided that an ongoing shift of guards would be at the school. It would be the beginning of a joint defense plan for the people of Sharidure and the Americans. Neither Ali nor Colonel Elliot believed the third attacker had left.

There was no attack that day, nor that night. Today was Saturday. Because of yesterday being Jumah, the day of worship, there had been no school. Today, school would be open. Ali watched the children, including his daughter Shireen and his son Hassan, come with their usual noisy selves. He counted the pairs of shoes outside the classrooms to see if there were students absent. Just one. Ali's wife Nafisa

Lori • By Howard Faber

and his sister Shireen joined the other teachers in starting the lessons. Everything seemed normal and quiet. He could hear Nafisa teaching reading.

In the afternoon, a

truck approached from the west. That was the usual arrival time for trucks from the west. Ali was on guard duty at that end of town. He approached the truck.

He stepped up to the truck to ask whether the driver had picked up any passengers on the road. He didn't recognize the driver. There were no passengers. Usually, there were passengers in the cab and in the back with the load. "Did you see anyone outside of town?"

"No."

Ali thought the man looked nervous. "What are you carrying?"

"Wheat."

The answers seemed very short. Something was wrong. The driver started toward town. Ali yelled to stop, but the truck kept going. Ali ran and grabbed onto the back. He pulled himself up onto the truck, crawled over the side of the truck, and moved around to the passenger side of the cab. He flung the door open and jumped into the cab. The driver saw him and swung his arm to try to hit him. Ali grabbed his arm and pulled him. The truck slowed some but kept going. The driver pulled away and leaned back toward the steering wheel. Ali decided to help him, pivoting on the seat and shoving the driver with both feet. The shove knocked the driver off balance and against the door. Ali scooted closer and gave another shove with both feet. That shove knocked the driver out of the door, and he tumbled down onto the road. Ali quickly sat up and grabbed the steering wheel, keeping the truck on the road.

There had to be a bomb on this truck. The driver probably had a cell phone to detonate it. He had to get the truck away from town or at least away from the school. He glanced in the side mirror to see what happened to the driver, if he had a cell phone, and was ready to blow up the truck. He saw him, but he was still on the ground, with an American soldier wrestling with him.

Ali thought quickly about where to drive the truck. Where was he now? Just where did the shops and homes start on main street. Where would there be no people? The old airfield. There would be no one there. He turned onto the side road that led to the old airfield. He didn't know what had happened now with the driver and the American. He sped up the hill toward the place where he played and where he landed the plane. The truck growled onto the old, still smooth landing strip. He drove it downhill toward the cliff overlooking the river valley, hoping for just a few seconds more.

His mind was racing again. Should he stop the truck and run? He could. If the American succeeded in controlling the bomber and prevented him from igniting the bomb, what would happen to the bomb. It might still hurt someone. He had to drive the truck off the cliff. The bomb would blow up as the truck crashed down in the valley. There were no roads down there so no one would be hurt. He decided to aim the truck for the cliff, stay in the truck until the last second, then jump out of the cab.

***

Back in Sharidure, the wrestling match was over. It turned out badly for the would-be bomber. The American soldier who jumped him was an All-American wrestler from Nebraska. He quickly pinned the man face first in the dirt. Two young men came running and now sat on the back of the attacker, each pinning an arm behind his back. The soldier radioed for help and Colonel Elliot came up in a Humvee.

The Talib looked very angry but helpless. He was now tied with rope, still face down in the dirt. The soldier quickly told Colonel Elliott about how this attacker tumbled down from a truck. "What happened to the truck?"

"I'm not too sure. I was pretty busy at the time." He said this with a wry smile. "I heard it start toward town, but then the sound faded away."

Ali slowed the truck, opened the cab door, and stepped sideways onto the side of the cab. He kept one hand on the steering wheel to keep the truck aimed at the cliff. When he took his foot off the gas pedal, the truck slowed quickly, and he thought for a second it might stop before going off the cliff, but because the landing strip was downhill, the truck kept going. He jumped off, landed on his feet, and watched it crawl forward. The front wheels rolled off the cliff, and the whole truck followed, bouncing once on the side of the cliff, then somersaulting into the air. Ali ran to the cliff's edge to watch. When it hit the valley floor, there was a huge explosion and fireball. Ali dropped to his knees and raised his hands.

When the people in Sharidure heard the huge explosion, they hurried toward the noise and smoke. Colonel Elliot drove his Humvee in that direction but had to slow down to avoid hitting the people running toward the river. When they rounded the side of the hill, they saw the burning truck. Everyone wondered if someone was in it, and how it had gotten there, since there was no road. Colonel Elliot left two of his soldiers there to find out as much as they could and to keep anyone from getting too close to the burning wreck. He went back to town to look for Ali to tell him about the Talib and the truck, but no one knew where Ali was.

Chapter Sixteen
A Time to Grow

Ali stayed at the edge of the cliff for a long time. He thought about his family at the school, now safe. He thought of his father, working at his shop, teaching him to be a carpenter, encouraging him to study. That seemed long ago. He thought about his for-a-time home in Iran, about returning to Afghanistan, about his wife, his sister. So many things, so many days. It was good to be home.

The clouds came and went, like the days that passed. He sat, looking out onto the river and its valley. He turned to look back to the top of the airfield, to where he had taken off and landed, remembering Dan and Reza, the two pilots, one American, one Iranian. He stood and started walking back up the airstrip, back home, back to where his mother made all of those meals, all of those clothes for him, encouraging him, telling him not to mind those mean boys who teased him about his leg. He had almost forgotten about his leg being bent for so long. Maybe there was a boy or girl now in Sharidure who needed a doctor and a hospital like he did. The Americans had a doctor with them.

As he started down the road from the airfield to town, he noticed a small figure starting up the road from town. As they each kept walking, they got close enough to recognize each other. "Baba (father), everyone is looking for you. Where have you been?" It was Hassan, his son.

"I was at the old airfield, thinking about how I used to come here, how the little plane used to land here. I was also thinking about another Hassan, your grandfather, and how he used to make me toys at his shop." They met on the little road, looked at each other a moment, then turned and walked hand-in-hand back to their home.

Someone saw Ali and hurried to Colonel Elliot to tell him where he was. When the American got to Ali's home, he asked Ali if he had found anything out about the third intruder.

"Please come in and have some tea. I did find out something about him. But first, please join me in my home."

Ali enjoyed seeing the colonel so much in a hurry to know. He also enjoyed knowing. He took his time but did start to tell about his encounter with the Talib in the truck, about driving it off the cliff, and seeing it explode below in the river valley. Hassan sat listening to the glorious story, seeing his dad so calm, so strong. It was a scene he would never forget or stop telling about.

Later that day, the two men, Ali and the colonel, told the story to their men. Hassan told it to his friends, who told it to their families. By evening, all of the people of Sharidure knew how Ali and the "palwahn," the American wrestler, saved their school and village from the Taliban attack. Ali told them about the additional hero, another Sharidure guard, who saved him from the second Talib up on the hill early that morning. He was anxious to meet the American soldier who wrestled and pinned the Talib into the dirt. They met early that afternoon. They shook hands and exchanged first names. The wrestler's name was Tom, and became known as "Mister Tom."

***

The next day Ali went to Colonel Elliot with a request.

"Could we build a hospital like we used to have? I can show you where it could be built. It would be a great help to us and to the other towns around us."

"That's part of what we hoped to do. We can start as soon as you want. Let's get Dr. Bettinga."

Dr. Bettinga was excited, almost as much as Ali, who explained how Sharidure used to have a hospital. He talked about both Doctors Hagel, about how he had an operation there to straighten his knee, and about how the hospital was so evilly smashed by the Taliban. They walked to where the hospital used to be. "How big was it? Did it have an operating room?"

"I think there were twelve rooms for patients. There was an operating room which had beautiful tile covering the walls, and a huge light balanced from the ceiling. I remember looking up at it, as I was lying on the table."

Ali went on to tell Dr. Bettinga about how many people would come in the summer to get medical help. "Even the Maldar would stop above town and pitch their tents, while they would get medical help from the Hagels. I was curious about them, but I didn't go very close because I was afraid of their big dogs."

"How did the doctors get their medicine?"

"Some came by road from Kabul, and some came by plane, a small plane. The place I drove the truck off the cliff was the airfield." These were some good memories, but Ali wanted to focus on getting a hospital for his town. "We could start work on our hospital tomorrow."

And tomorrow it was. The soldiers had cement and the men of Sharidure had the muscle. One of the American soldiers was an engineer. Ali showed him the foundations of the old hospital. The engineer thought they could still use those for the new one, and there were plenty of large stones for the walls.

The day after that, a helicopter arrived with more supplies for the hospital. It landed on the old airfield, where Colonel Elliot and Dr. Bettinga were waiting to supervise the unloading. They invited Ali to ride with them. Hassan heard about the helicopter coming and wanted to see it, and Ali was happy to have him so interested. When the helicopter flew in, all the other children of Sharidure ran to the airfield to see it. When it was unloaded, the pilot agreed to take Ali and

Colonel Elliot up for a short ride. Hassan asked if he and his sister could go too. The pilot helped the children buckle their seat belts, and it was a glorious ride.

Hassan and Shireen got a birds-eye view of their home. "Look, there's our house, and there's the school!" Hassan shouted because of the engine noise.

"Everything looks so small. Where does that road go? Does it go to Bamiyan?" Shireen knew about Bamiyan and the ancient Buddhas.

"Yes, Bamiyan is over there." Ali pointed east. "We'll go to see the Buddhas, when the road is safe."

When they landed at the airfield, Colonel Elliot helped Shireen and Hassan down. All the children cheered and secretly wished they too could go up in the helicopter. Their hopes grew two sizes that day.

There were lots of changes that summer. The first one was the little room at the airfield. It soon became two big rooms with windows, a sloping roof to keep snow out in the winter, a radio, two stoves (one for each room), and a small radar. The Sharidure airfield had a significant upgrade.

The hospital was next. It was finished in about a month,

complete with a pharmacy, several examination rooms, a comfortable office, an x-ray room, twelve rooms for hospitalized patients, and a modern, sparkling clean surgery, complete with an overhead light like Ali remembered. Dr. Bettinga made sure that this was a hospital to be proud of. He saw many patients each day and kept the pharmacy supplied with the necessary medicine. The next month, they build an additional wing, designed for new mothers and babies. Dr. Bettinga found a newly graduated Afghan doctor to help him. She specialized in seeing the female patients. He was very busy seeing men and boys.

The American soldiers worked in eight-hour shifts, alongside the now larger Sharidure group of guards. They checked each vehicle coming to town and required each person not from the village to be interviewed and searched.

When not on duty, the Americans had a special project as their focus, the school. They made wooden desks, larger chalkboards, added classrooms, and put glass and screens in the windows. They saw fifty students in a classroom and decided more classrooms were needed, so they built more rooms on the school, each one having lights. That was possible because the engineer built a small electricity-producing power plant upstream from Sharidure. The school and hospital got the first power lines. There were plans to add another generator and more power lines.

Next to the school was a new volleyball court, which became a gathering place for the town. On Wednesday evenings, there were matches where everyone cheered, laughed, and felt proud of their town. A grandstand was built on one side of the court, facing a sidewall of the school with the volleyball court in between. The supply helicopters brought a projector, and the Sharidure outdoor theater was born. Ahmroodeen was the master of ceremonies and translator for the shows, mostly children's videos. Elmo became a favorite.

***

At the end of summer, Colonel Elliot stopped by Ali and Nafisa's home to ask for his help. "Could you come with me to the American base near Kabul to talk to my commander about Sharidure and the possibility of repeating what you have done here in other communities in this area?"

It was Nafisa who answered first. "Of course, Ali should

Kodamon Valley • By Howard Faber

go. We are proud of our hometown. We would like others to experience what we have here."

It was decided that Ali, Colonel Elliot, and Ahmroodeen would go the next day to Bagram, the American base. They rode in a humvee, stopping first at the beautiful lakes, Bondi-Amir, then in Bamiyan. Ali just shook his head sadly at the sight of the ruined Buddhas.

They kept going, over the pass, then gradually down toward the road into Kabul.

It took all day, so it was almost dark when they

approached the huge base. The base guards knew they were coming, so security was thorough but quick, and they were warmly welcomed by Colonel Elliot's commander.

Ali, Colonel Elliot, and Ahmroodeen were his guests at a big dinner. The amount of food was mind-boggling, though there were just six people in the room, the three from Sharidure, and three American officers. Eventually, the talk came around to what was accomplished in Sharidure. "We would like to see your home." This was from the man who seemed to be the leader of the soldiers, a General Ridder. "How long does the trip take?"

"It took twelve hours on the way down. We stopped twice. The road is not made for very fast travel." Colonel Elliot wasn't sure the general had traveled lately in a Humvee.

"Do you know if there are any small planes available?" Ali was thinking about the airfield at Sharidure. "There's a small airfield just above the town. A small plane flew there every week. I know the way by air."

The Americans talked for a minute. "Yes, there is a small plane a private group uses. We have used it before. Let's leave in the morning."

Early in the morning Ali was flying back to Sharidure, telling the pilot the best route, and about the small airfield. The plane was the same size that Dan and Ali flew what now seemed so long ago. They flew over Bamiyan and the Buddhas.

General Ridder had never seen them. Ali tried to explain how they used to look. There was a lot in Afghanistan that

Bamiyan Valley • UNO

used to look beautiful, but not now. Soon, the deep blue lakes of Bondi Amir were below them. The pilot circled to see them better. Ali was now looking ahead to see his home. He explained to the pilot that he could follow the river, then circle once to line up with the small runway. The pilot wanted to fly over it once to get a better idea of how it was. When they flew over the river next to Sharidure the sound of the plane got everybody's attention. Ali asked the pilot to waggle the wings, a signal for Shireen, his sister, so she would know Ali was in the plane and not to worry.

"It's a beautiful, peaceful place," Ahmroodeen said as he translated both General Ridder's words and tone.

"Thank you. It's my home." Ali thought about his home, as the pilot circled the plane up and away from the river to line up with the small airfield of Sharidure. He thought about his flights with Dan, the pilot who helped him learn to fly, about the small hospital where Dr. Hagen changed his life from a crutch to standing on two feet, about his parents, and about his sister Shireen, his early protector.

After they landed, his thoughts came back to the present, to his wife and children, and protecting his home and town. There they were, his family, Nafisa, Hassan, Shireen and Shireen. Hassan and little Shireen ran and skipped up to greet him. He introduced them to the American general. General Ridder had gifts for them, a baseball cap for Hassan and a backpack for Shireen. He had done his homework.

The next day, after much planning, and much hopeful talk, Ali waved goodbye to General Ridder as the plane started down the runway. He walked back down the path to Sharidure, going home. As he walked, he thought back to his life here, growing up, his parents, his operation, school, friends, these were the good things. He also thought about when he left, the fear, the uncertainty. Now, he was back, and it was the right place for him and for his family. This was his home, a place he fought for, and if need be would fight again. It was no longer a faraway home.

Characters

Ahmad Nabi
Husband of Ali's sister Shireen

Ahmroodeen
Translator with the U. S. Special Forces

Akbar
Hassan's friend in Mashed

Ali
Main character

Anisa
Akbar's wife

Askgar
Head of mujahedeen in Sharidure

Bibi Jan
Ali's father's mother

Colonel Elliot
American special forces

Dan
the American pilot

Doctor Hagel
Male American doctor

Doctor Hagel
Female American doctor

Dr. Bettinga
Medical officer with the US Special Forces

Farid
Hassan's cousin in Kabul

Hassan
Ali and Nafisa's son

Hassan
Ali's father

Homyoon
Substitute Iranian pilot

Hossein
Friend of Ali growing up

Mariam
Ali's mother

Mohammad
Akbar's son

Naeem
Bamiyan truck driver

Nafisa
Ali's wife

Reza
Iranian pilot

Sara
Akbar's daughter

Sayeed
Carpenter in Muhshed (Ali's father-in-law)

Shireen
Ali and Nafisa's daughter

Shireen
Ali's older sister

Tom
American soldier (All-American wrestler from Nebraska)

Dari Words and Phrases

aash - noodle and vegetable soup

bisyar khoub - very good

kharbooza- sweet melon

koochi / maldar - nomad

leeoff - long floor cushion

Qauzi - Islamic judge

shafakhona - hospital

Shia - one of the main Islamic groups

Sunni - one of the main Islamic groups

tope danda - ball game

Places and Names

Bamiyan - city and province in the area of the Hazara

Bondi-Amir - series of lakes

Buddha - two huge statues in Bamiyan

Chaghcharan - town in central Afghanistan

Chengis Khan - ancient mongol ruler who conquered Afghanistan

Hazara - Afghan cultural group

Hazarajat - area of the Hazara people

Islam Qala - small town on Afghan / Iranian border

Kabul - Afghan capital

Muhshed - eastern Iranian city

Nooristan - area in Afghanistan

Salang tunnel - tunnel connecting Kabul with the north

Sharidure - fictitious town

Shebar Pass - pass between Kabul and Bamiyan

Tyabad - Iranian border town

Author's Bio

This is about me and about how I came to write this story. My wife is a retired high school principal. I teach fifth and sixth graders. Our daughter is in college. My education came first on our farm, and continues in lots of ways. My college degrees are from the University of Northern Iowa (BA), Columbia University (MA), and the University of Nebraska (EdD).

I've taught since 1965, taking off two years when I was in the US Army. My first teaching jobs were in Kabul, Afghanistan, initially with the Peace Corps in an Afghan high school, and later with schools primarily for children of foreign families living in Kabul.

For two summers, I worked as a volunteer with a medical group that cared for the people of central Afghanistan, the setting for this story. I met the main character, Ali, in the town that I call Sharidure. He did have a bent knee. He used to race other kids along the tops of the many walls in the town. The doctors later straightened his knee.

Except for the army and graduate school, I lived in Afghanistan from 1965 to 1975. The closest I've gotten back to Afghanistan was to go to Peshawer, Pakistan for two summers in the early 1990s to write textbooks for Afghan children.

Acknowledgements

I would like to thank the University of Nebraska at Omaha Center for Afghan Studies for some of the photos. Other photos are compliments of people who I worked with in Afghanistan.

The name of Ali's town, Sharidure, was suggested by Yasir, a friend who works at UNO.

I also want to thank David Martin, who encouraged me to publish this story, and who did the initial editing.

Howard Faber